CW00515488

Dawson Fur Hire

Dawson Fur Hire
ISBN-13: 978-1533293145
ISBN-10: 1533293147
Copyright © 2016, T. S. Joyce
First electronic publication: January 2016

T. S. Joyce
www.tsjoyce.com

All Rights Are Reserved. No part of this book may be used or reproduced in any manner whatsoever without written permission, except in the case of brief quotations embodied in critical articles and reviews. The unauthorized reproduction or distribution of this copyrighted work is illegal. No part of this book may be scanned, uploaded or distributed via the Internet or any other means, electronic or print, without the author's permission.

NOTE FROM THE AUTHOR:
This book is a work of fiction. The names, characters, places, and incidents are products of the writer's imagination or have been used fictitiously and are not to be construed as real. Any resemblance to persons, living or dead, actual events, locale or organizations is entirely coincidental. The author does not have any control over and does not assume any responsibility for third-party websites or their content.

Published in the United States of America
First digital publication: January 2016
First print publication: May 2016

Dawson Fur Hire

(Bears Fur Hire, Book 5)

T. S. Joyce

ONE

Dalton Dawson narrowed his eyes at the smell of werewolf that traveled in on the frigid breeze through the bar's open front door. Maybe if he ignored his alpha, Link would get the hint and leave him the hell alone.

Gritting his teeth, he glared up at the local weather report on the small television behind the bar and emptied his whiskey on the rocks. Beside him, Link slid onto the barstool and pulled his gloves off slowly, one by one. Dalton could feel Link staring at him.

"What?"

"Chance called."

Dalton swallowed a growl and lifted his finger to the bartender, asking for another.

"How many drinks is that?"

"A million."

"He told me, Dalton." Link swallowed audibly and lowered his voice. "He told me about April First."

"Well, Chance is a dick, and now I'm going to kick his ass," Dalton muttered under his breath.

"What I can't figure out is how I didn't know about this before now." Despite Link's rigid profile, he smiled politely to the bartender who was setting yet another whiskey in front of Dalton. "I'll have what he's having." His alpha looked tired, his black hair mussed, his gray eyes dull, but that's what happened with a new baby.

Pain slashed through Dalton's chest. He would give anything to feel that kind of exhaustion now. It would mean that April First had never happened.

"Why are you here, Link? Your responsibility is with Nicole and Fina."

"And you."

"What?" Dalton made a single click behind his teeth and shook his head. "Our pack doesn't work like that. I live near Kodiak with Chance. We deal with our own shit. I only come here when I need town. You aren't responsible for me."

"Bullshit, you come here when your wolf drives you to. And as for us not working like a real pack…" He jacked up his dark eyebrows and leveled him with a look. "That's not what I want. It's not how I want us to function. It's really fucked up that I've been your alpha for over a year now, and I didn't know about April First. You could've leaned on me, man."

"Stop it. Can't you see? I'm not here asking for attention. I came here to hide out in your old cabin for a few days and escape Chance's worried momma hen looks. I don't need you picking up where that tattling fucker left off."

"He's worried—"

"I don't care."

"Chance is worried and so am I. I've never seen you drink more than Vera's homemade beer, and you're in here throwing whiskey back like it's water. Look around, Dalton. This place is one hundred percent human, and your eyes are glowing. I don't know if you've heard yourself lately, or if you even notice it right now, but you've been growling the entire time I've been here. You aren't a McCall. You're a Dawson. Don't attract Clayton's attention."

Dalton swallowed the snarl that he hadn't in fact noticed until Link pointed it out. "Why, because it'll look bad on you?"

"No, you dumbass. Because I don't want to go to war with Clayton because of one drunken night in a bar."

Well, that drew Dalton up short. Link would go to war with the head of the Shifter Enforcement Agency for him? Dalton stared at Link as he downed his whiskey. Huh. They didn't see each other much on account of him living near Kodiak where he worked as an outdoor guide and Link living here in Galena, but Dalton suddenly understood. Link could be a good alpha.

Ha! A McCall being a good alpha? He must be drunker than he thought.

Link had taken over their pack of two to save himself from going mad. This was a pack of convenience, nothing more. "Go home, McCall. I'm fine. I promise I won't make a scene." Dalton scanned the full bar. "I just need to get my dick stroked, and this will all be easier."

"My wolf used to tell me that when I was in the desperate procreation phase of madness."

"Well, I'm not a McCall."

"No," Link murmured, turning a lightened gaze on him. "You're better. Call me if you need a ride home." He slammed back his shot and made to stand, but hesitated and patted the wooden bar top. "Before I forget. Nicole wants you to come over for dinner tomorrow night."

"Why?"

"Because like it or not, she loves you and Chance. And I know this can't be easy. I *know*. I've had losses, too, Dalton, but the fact is, we're a pack, and we have a new pup in the family. You and Chance should both spend time with Fina when you're in town."

"Nice, man. Chance told you about April First, and your solution is to have me come see your baby girl?"

"No, Chance told me this much"—Link held his finger and thumb an inch apart—"about April First. You can tell me the rest when you're ready. And yeah, I want my kid knowing her people. Dinner is at six."

Her people. Dalton stared in shock as Link snatched his gloves off the counter, threw down a ten dollar bill, and strode from the bar. Dalton hadn't held Fina, *for a reason*, but he was her people? That's not how this was supposed to work. Sure, he'd visited Galena with Chance a couple times when Nicole was pregnant. Why? Because he thought being around to support Link would help his alpha deal with the fact that his mate might lose a little baby girl.

He knew all about those kinds of scars. Females werewolves didn't survive past a couple days after birth, but Vera-the-mouthy-mad-scientist had promised she would try to cure that issue. She'd made the oath to try, but still, Dalton hadn't really believed she could do it. Sure, she'd cured the bear shifters' hibernation instincts and even cured Link of his fucked-up McCall genetics, but fixing the gene that killed baby female werewolves? He still couldn't believe Link's daughter, Fina, was still here, thriving, at three months old.

But even in the wake of Vera's cures, in the small amount of time he'd spent in Galena to lend Link and his mate support, he had never been mistaken about what this pack really was. His wolf had bowed to Link because Dalton had forced it to. He was submissive to Link because he and Chance had chosen to put themselves under him in exchange for Vera curing female babies. Sure, Link was a beast and plenty dominant to run this pack, but so were he and Chance. They weren't stunted McCalls like Link's last pack. He, Chance, and Link were all brawler werewolves and dominant. Link was alpha, but only because Dalton and Chance allowed him to be.

This wasn't a real pack.

Dalton slammed another whiskey. It wasn't. *Wasn't.*

He couldn't afford to get close to people. Couldn't afford to let Link, Nicole, and Fina in.

Not after April First.

When the door opened behind him, the subtle smell of honey replaced the werewolf scent. Intrigued, Dalton twisted around in his chair, then froze when he saw the woman who stood timidly in the doorway.

He'd never seen anyone look so out of place. She lifted bright green eyes from the floor, chin to her chest as she tugged a pink scarf from her neck. When she pulled back the hood to her winter coat, shoulder-length waves of strawberry red hair tumbled around her neck. She was small, mousey almost, with a little pixie nose, tiny glossed lips, and eyes almost too big for her face. Or maybe they were that big because she was frightened. The faint scent of fear backed up that theory. She was a beauty, to be sure, but he pitied her for her weakness as she inched along the wall, avoiding contact with the laughing, joking bar patrons.

What the hell was a woman like her doing in Alaska? This wasn't exactly a landscape for the faint of heart, and she looked like prey. Beautiful, fuckable prey. Another soft snarl rattled his chest, and he swallowed it down with another whiskey. This bartender was a good one and didn't ask questions. The old, grizzled man just kept them coming.

"She's a looker, ain't she?" a bearded man a couple bar stools down asked.

Dalton gave him a glare, then nodded once. "She's all right."

"She ain't poor either. She's got a steady job as one of them nurses down at the medical center. Brains to go with her beauty. And," he drawled, clutching his beer and leaning closer to Dalton, "she's a wildcat in the bedroom."

Dalton gritted his teeth. He wanted to rip this asshole's heart through his chest cavity for talking about her like that, but for the life of him, he didn't know why. This lady didn't need saving from a spiraling werewolf.

Unable to help himself, Dalton ripped his glare away from the man's expectant dark eyes to the woman again. She'd stripped out of her jacket to a pair of pink scrubs, not exactly the jeans and tight, tit-baring bar attire the trio of boozing ladies near the bathroom were wearing.

"Her name's Katherine Hawke. She goes by Kate," the man beside him slurred. "You know what they say about Kates. It's all true. I have proof."

Dalton ignored him in favor of watching the woman sidle up to a pool table where a pair of tatted-up men were playing a game.

Kate. He didn't know what people said about Kates, but he liked the name on her. His inner wolf did, too, because he had stopped the incessant snarling and gone blissfully silent.

"I want to play you," Kate said to the tallest of the good old boys in a voice no louder than a murmur.

11

Thank God for his oversensitive hearing.

The man glared at Kate. "Fuck off."

Dalton forced himself to stay seated and not blur across the room and put that prick through the wall.

Kate slapped down a few bills. Twenties if his eyes weren't playing tricks on him. That was wealth around here.

The man stared at the money laid on the green felt of the table with a calculating look. He slid his bearded jaw back and forth thoughtfully, then dragged a hate-filled glare to Kate. She wilted a bit under his scrutiny, but stood her ground.

"We're playing doubles."

"I just want to play you."

"Fine, bitch. You rack. I don't want you snapping your puny arm off trying to break."

"Put your money down first." Her voice shook, and it was all Dalton could do not to go rescue her from the bad decision she was making.

The loaded moment dragged on and on, but finally, Blockhead slapped down cash right next to her stack, then started chalking up his pool stick. "Brett, go get us a pitcher, will you?"

Brett made his way toward the bar, and while he put in his order, Dalton paid his tab. He couldn't stick around to watch this. She was a grown woman, and he wasn't in any position to help anyone. He couldn't even help himself right now.

Kate racked the balls like she'd done it before, slow but steady, and then she stood back to allow Blockhead to break. Which he did and nearly blasted one of the balls off the table. A couple went in the pockets, and he put a couple more in before he missed. With a dark chuckle, he said, "Good luck, bitch."

Dalton needed to leave now. If he heard the word "bitch" said to her again, he was going to lose his mind. He pocketed his wallet and grabbed his jacket from the chair beside him, but the crack of the pool balls drew him up short. He watched in utter shock as Kate bent over gracefully and sank another solid into the corner pocket, then lined up another shot. Ball after ball, she hit where she intended until all that was left was a difficult eight-ball shot, which she banked into the side pocket. What the hell?

"Sexy ass shark," the man beside him muttered. Then the whoosh of a rubber cell phone cover sounded as it slid across the bar top. "Take a look at this. She might be timid, but she's a little freak in the sheets."

Blinking back his bafflement at Kate snatching the cash off the table, Dalton turned to find a video playing on the man's cell. The volume was all the way up and moaning sex sounds emanated from the device. Dalton stared in horror as a woman was fucked from behind, pale skin glowing in the dim lighting of a bedroom, boobs bouncing under her, strawberry-colored waves hiding her face as she arched her back for the man behind her. Slowly, the man turned to face the screen, a wicked grin twisting his lips as though he knew the camera was there. Oh, shit. Dalton recognized that man. No, he recognized that *monster*. Timid pool shark, Kate, was getting a good doggy-style banging from Miller McCall.

A tiny gasp sounded behind him, and Dalton rolled his eyes closed and gritted his teeth with regret.

"Hey, wildcat," the asshole with the phone porn said unapologetically.

When Dalton turned, Kate was standing right behind him. Her cheeks were the color of cherries, and her eyes had somehow grown even bigger. Her mortified look gutted him. "I didn't—I didn't mean to…"

"Watch that horrible video?" she whispered.

Kate looked from him to the phone still blaring out her moans. In it, she was about to come if the noises she was making were any indication. Dalton pulled his jacket in front of his boner. He hated seeing Miller covering her, but she sounded so damned sexy he couldn't help it. His dick was betraying him bad right now.

Even deeper hurt filled her eyes as she dared a look back up at Dalton, then dropped them to the ground again. "So you know," she whispered, "I didn't know that video was taken." Shame tainted every word, and each one felt like a blow to his stomach.

"I'm sorry."

"Yeah, I bet you are." She lifted her chin to the bartender and took a flask from him, then gave him a twenty dollar bill. "Keep it, Jerry."

"I sure appreciate it, Kate," the bartender said softly.

She nodded once, tossed Dalton another embarrassed glance, then left in a hurry.

Seething, Dalton took the damning phone and dropped it in the prick's beer to stop the sound of Kate's orgasm.

"Hey!" the man yelled, fishing for it with his meaty fingers. "That's my phone! I did you a favor showing you that, and this is how you repay me? Shit." He upended the drink onto the bar top.

"If you play that video ever again," Dalton gritted out low, "I'm going to find you and I'm going to rip your fucking throat out."

"His name is Bart Mathews," Jerry the Bartender offered helpfully.

Dalton gave him a venomous smile. "Don't test me, Bart. I'm a man of my word and itchin' to bleed someone."

"Anyone can see it, man! It's online. Her damn name is tagged on it and everything." Bart jammed the on button over and over, but the screen stayed blank. "Now my phone won't turn on!"

Dalton strode for the door, desperate to escape before he picked a fight with Bart, Blockhead, and the rest of the damned bar. There was no keeping his wolf quiet now. His inner animal was scrabbling to escape his skin.

When Blockhead elbowed his way out the door first, Dalton nearly lost it at the smell of potent fury washing from his pungent skin.

Tonight, that timid woman had been called names and humiliated publicly, and Dalton had been a part of that. He wanted to double over in the late season snow and retch.

A throaty four-wheeler engine revved at the far side of the parking lot. Kate hit the throttle on the fat-tired ATV and blasted out of her parking spot. He could've sworn she wiped her eyes before she turned onto the main road in town. God, he felt like grit.

You should apologize and then have sex with her.

Dalton ground out an irritated sound for his wolf's unhelpful suggestion and hopped onto his snow machine. When he turned on the engine, exhaust fumes smoked around him. Canting his head in the direction she'd driven off, he considered his wolf's suggestion, though. Chicks liked apologies. At least, his ex, Shelby, had. She'd liked apologies all the time because the only thing she liked more than always being right was him admitting he was wrong.

Or if he didn't talk to Kate again, at least his curiosity was piqued. A timid nurse by day and a flask-guzzling pool shark by night was a study in opposites and a sweet little distraction from his April First anniversary issues right now.

His wolf could use a little hunt.

Before he could change his mind, Dalton hit the throttle and followed the fading taillights. It was late, and Galena was a ghost town right now, so he cut the lights and followed in the dark. His night vision was impeccable, and he could see everything just fine without them.

He followed far behind and parked on a side street when she pulled to a stop in front of a small home with lavender siding. He hid behind a thick grove of bushes. The home was nice enough, but she disappeared down a short set of stairs to a dilapidated basement entrance, and it looked like she was being quiet about it. A few minutes inside, and she came back out, holding an envelope and closing the door slowly and softly before she locked it back up. She gave a quick, suspicious glance around, then shoved the roughed-up money from her game of pool into the envelope and licked it closed. Then she pulled on her gloves and jogged across a couple of snowy front yards to a house with sage green siding. Another glance around, and she shoved the envelope of money into the mail slot on the front door.

What the hell? Maybe she was into drugs or something.

Another couple houses down down, and she knocked softly on the door of a small cottage with chipped paint and a sagging roof. An older woman answered the door, and Kate handed her the flask she'd taken from the bar. The woman's wrinkled face lit up, and she gave Kate's shoulders a big squeeze. Easing back, the woman gripped Kate's arm with shaking, gnarled fingers as she hugged the flask to her chest with the other hand.

Dalton shook his head. She was a nurse, and she was enabling an alcoholic?

Maybe he'd pegged her wrong. Maybe she wasn't timid at all. The facts were she had conned Blockhead out of his hard-earned money, had a sex tape with Miller McCall, the late alpha of the man-eating McCall pack, and was into a sketchy delivery service out here in the middle of the night.

His curiosity needed to end right here and right now.

Even if he was looking, which he wasn't, Kate Hawke would make a terrible mate.

And he'd already been there, done that.

TWO

Kate's cheeks heated with pleasure as she said goodbye to Mrs. Tanner. She would do more than just get booze for her if she needed it. That woman was one of the only people she trusted outside of her family. To trust someone was a huge deal for Kate, and she could count on one hand the number of folks she had faith in.

She gave Mrs. Tanner a wave and told her, "You call me if you need any more." Then she turned to walk back to her basement apartment. The night was quiet except for the distant drone of a truck approaching. Her boots crunched satisfyingly against the untouched snow as she made her way across the neighbors' yards. It was better than taking the icy sidewalk.

It was the first of April, and warmer temperatures would be here soon, so she was enjoying the last of the crisp weather. She liked winter best. Summers were beautiful with all the mosses, ferns, leafy alders, and warm weather. But it also brought the bugs and the mud.

She looked up to wave politely to the passing truck because that's what people did in Galena. It was one of the things she loved about living in a small town. Everyone knew everyone, and the nice ones formed a loose-knit web of care for each other. The greeting smile faded from her face when she saw who it was.

Darren skidded to a stop, his truck halfway in her yard. Shoot. With a gasp, she bolted for the safety of her apartment, but judging from his speed, the drunkard was motivated. "Where are you going, bitch?"

She hated that name. Hated him. He was awful to everyone. He was running now, cutting straight for her, and she yelped as he grabbed the sleeve of her coat and shook her hard enough to rattle her bones.

"You think you're so smart, don't you? I know what you did. It took me a minute, but I know. Fuckin' hero." He shoved her onto the ground and reared back to kick her.

With a squeak of terror, she curled in on herself and covered her ears, closed her eyes, elbows and knees in, just like Miller had taught her to do before he'd disappeared. Protect the vitals.

But right when she'd expected him to connect with her middle, Darren grunted in a sound that was shock and pain all at once. And when she opened one eye, he was gone. Just…gone.

Stunned, she sat up in the snow and scanned the yard. No, not gone, just way the heck over there, and he was getting his ass kicked by someone. A tall man sat straddled over Darren's bulbous gut, pummeling his face so fast he seemed to blur. Kate stood just as the man lifted Darren off the ground like he weighed nothing at all.

She gasped. Holy crap. She'd seen strength like that before. She'd felt it.

The man's back was to her when he chucked Darren across two yards. He landed hard on the snowy ground and slid the length of another yard. Kate stood as frozen as an ice sculpture when the man turned his face, offering only his profile. "Get inside," he said in a gravelly voice.

Darren struggled to his feet and looked like a pissed-off bull.

Her defender looked familiar, but he wore a hat over his hair, and his face had transformed into something fearsome. Still, he resembled the stranger at the bar, the man who'd been watching that awful video Miller had posted. The damning video that had nearly ruined her life and demolished her pride.

"Move now," the man barked as Darren charged.

"Okay," she rushed out, bolting for the door to her basement home.

Darren was scary and a violent drunk, but this guy didn't seem to have any problem beating the crap out of him so he was probably okay on his own. Still, Darren was a behemoth and didn't feel much when he was drinking. She unlocked her door with a sense of panicked urgency, careful to be quiet so she didn't wake up Mr. Harris, her landlord who lived in the main house above. He didn't sleep well at nights—insomnia, just like her—so she tried to be considerate. Still, her keys jingled in her shaking hands and sounded loud in the quiet night. That was until Darren started cussing. The sound of fists connecting with skin scared her. That stranger was trying to help her, and he was going to get hurt on her account.

As soon as her door was open, she bolted for the small corner kitchen at the back of her one-room apartment, grabbed the first heavy object she could use as a weapon, then sprinted back up the stairs and onto the lawn. She charged the fight, but skidded to a stop as the stranger lifted

Darren off the ground by his jacket and gritted out something too low for her to hear.

Darren's face went slack, and he nodded. "Okay, man. I won't. I'll leave."

The man shoved Darren away, who stumbled backward, barely managing to stay upright. Darren turned and limped to his truck without a single look back. Her protector hooked his hands on his hips as Darren revved his engine and sped off, fishtailing down the icy street as he went.

"I told you to go inside," the man said without turning around.

I know what you are. The words were right there on her tongue, but she couldn't bring herself to say them out loud. She'd learned the hard way monsters like him guarded their secrets. She'd only survived Miller by pretending to be naïve.

The man turned toward her, and he blinked a surprised look at the iron skillet she held above her head. "What are you doing with that?"

"I was going to save you."

He snorted, but pursed his lips and looked off into the woods at the end of the street.

"Clearly you don't need the help," she murmured, lowering her weapon. "What are you doing here?"

The man cocked his head in a very animal-like gesture, and his scotch-colored eyes glinted strangely in the glow of the porch light Mr. Harris always kept on for her. He looked dangerous. Dark hair stuck out from under his navy winter hat, and his cheekbones were sharp. Even his eyes looked like they belonged on an animal. Slanted, calculating…stunning. His features were exotic, and his skin was an olive tone as though he'd been out in the sun. Perhaps he was Alaska Native.

"I'm here to apologize for…you know."

"Watching a porno of me?"

He cleared his throat and scrunched up his face, then nodded. "Yeah, that. I didn't ask to see it. Bart pulled it up…" The man gritted his teeth, then spat red onto the snow by his feet. Apparently he'd taken a hit. "My name is Dalton Dawson."

A handsome name for a handsome man, but he was still dangerous. Even from across the lawn, the fine hairs all over her body had electrified at how heavy he felt. Miller had felt like that, too, only she hadn't known any better. At the time, she hadn't figured out he was a monster yet.

"Thank you for keeping Darren off me." Her cheeks flushed so hot she dropped her gaze to the toe of his boot in embarrassment. "We're even now. Apology accepted."

"Why are you holding the skillet like that?"

Kate looked down to her stomach where she was holding it like a small shield. *Because you're a werewolf.* "I don't know."

"Are you hurt?"

"No, I'm fine. He grabbed my jacket. Missed my meaty parts." She let off a lame, nervous laugh.

"Are you scared of me?"

Her voice would shake if she answered, so instead, she braved a glance at him and nodded her head in a jerk.

"I won't hurt you." His voice sounded confident, full of conviction, as if he believed he would really never hurt her.

Sadness heavy in her heart, she forced a smile. "Everyone hurts me. Have a good night, Dalton Dawson."

She descended the five stairs to her basement apartment and opened the door.

"Kate?" he asked.

She turned slowly. "Yes?"

"Why was that man after you? What kind of trouble are you in?"

She shrugged helplessly. Darren would always be after her because she cared. "He bullied his mom for that money. She's my neighbor. Nice lady who would give the clothes off her back in the middle of winter if somebody needed it.

He takes advantage. She wouldn't be able to pay her rent this month without that money, but Darren doesn't worry about other people. He's a taker. I knew he would be in the bar tonight wasting his mom's rent money, so I won it back."

"And then you gave it back to her in that envelope?"

He'd been watching her. Carefully, she nodded.

"And the flask?"

She inhaled slowly, then exhaled her crystallizing breath. She didn't like answering to a stranger, but he'd saved her from Darren's brutal boots. "Mrs. Tanner has rheumatoid arthritis, but she doesn't like taking medicine. She says only whiskey makes her feel better. She drinks it to take the edge off, but a flask usually lasts her a couple of weeks. She's tough."

Dalton swallowed hard and crossed his arms over his chest. "Let me guess. She doesn't have money for whiskey?"

Kate shook her head. "I have a good job. I can help."

Dalton's eyes looked darker now, more Guinness than whiskey. He made her heart pound hard in her chest, staring at her like this, trapping her with his gaze. She had to be careful with him. Miller had looked at her like this, too. Possessive, like she was his. Animals did that—collected mates like trophies. She would never be a trophy again.

Dalton sighed a long, frozen breath. He looked lethal in the dim porch light. Back straight, arms crossed, wide shoulders fighting against the fabric of his coat, long legs tensed. He could be over the yard and to her in a moment.

She waved nervously and slid in through the open door, then locked the deadbolt behind her. She fought the urge to turn on the light. He might see her silhouette through the thin curtains, and this way, she could sneak the blind open, and it wouldn't be obvious she was spying on him.

A mixture of mortification and intrigue washed through her as she watched his profile through the slightly lifted blind. He'd seen that horrible video Miller had uploaded onto the internet, but then he'd come and protected her. Miller had never protected her from anything. He liked her hurt, but this man, Dalton, had kept Darren from kicking her, and then asked if she was hurt. And he'd seemed bothered by her admission that she was scared of him.

But he was a werewolf, and experience with Miller and his A-hole brothers said they were never to be trusted. Never.

Dalton linked his hands behind his head in the front yard. "Shit," he muttered just loud enough for her to hear. Shaking his head, he approached her door, but before he knocked, he sat down in the snow on the top stair of her stoop.

Confused, she let the plastic blind fall back into place and stared at the door with a frown. Why was he getting comfortable like he was settling in for the night? He was probably off his rocker.

She readied for bed, all the while lost in swirling thoughts of his reasons for protecting her. Dressed in her warm pajama pants and a sweater to ward off the cold of the basement, she brushed her teeth and washed her face, then padded back to the front door out of curiosity. Steeling herself, she lifted the blind again. Dalton was still there, arms draped over his knees and staring toward the street. It was really cold out there.

It would be impossible for her to sleep tonight. Her time with Miller had done that—made her too afraid to let her body go unconscious for long—and now she would be lying in bed wondering about Dalton's motives for sitting by her apartment in the snow.

Determined to shoo him away, she flipped on the light, then opened the door a crack. "What are you still doing here?"

"Standing guard, making sure that asshole doesn't come back after I leave."

"You don't have to do that."

"Apparently I have to. My…something inside of me won't let me leave."

She narrowed her eyes. "Hmmm." He was very different from Miller. Dalton's inner animal seemed protective, not brutal.

She shut the door and locked it, then pulled the thick blanket off the back of her couch and opened the door again. Hesitating only a moment, she tossed him the blanket. "If you must stay, I can't stand the thought of you being cold."

He held up the red quilt and nodded. "I appreciate it." Blood was drying on his lip, and he favored his jaw when he spoke. She hoped it wasn't broken.

She brought him a bag of frozen peas from her freezer and gestured to his mouth. "For where Darren hit you."

Dalton stared at her for too long, but finally took the peas, held them up in a silent *thank you*, then pressed it onto his jaw.

But that would make him colder, so she went to work and made him a thermos of hot chocolate. She crept up the stairs carefully and set the metal mug next to him. That was as close as she'd ever been to the man, a test, but he didn't try to grab her. He thanked her through a half-smile instead.

She closed the door again. He would probably get bored. She pulled a magazine off her coffee table and climbed the stairs again, daring to get even closer to hand it to him.

"This looks super girly," he murmured, frowning down at her offering.

"There's a quiz on page thirty-six about soulmates and another about the perfect nail polish color for you. I can bring you a pencil if you want."

From here, a few stairs below, she was almost eye-level with him. He was even sexier up-close, and she was trapped again in his striking gaze.

"Invite me in," he said low.

"You're not a vampire," she joked, but heat burned her cheeks when she realized how close she'd gotten to exposing just how much she knew about wolf-people like him.

"No, but you'll fuss over me all night if I don't come in. I won't hurt you. I'll watch over you tonight, then be out of your life tomorrow."

"I have a couch."

"I'll keep you safe."

Kate let off a long, shaky sigh. Safe. That sounded nice after everything that had happened over the last few years. "Swear."

"I swear," he said, void of hesitation.

She looked back to her partially open door, considering his offer. She didn't feel safe when she slept, and now she was inviting a stranger into her home. Sure, he'd protected her from Darren and he was sitting in the freezing cold now watching over her, but still.

"I'm not like that video," she said, giving him a harsh look. "If that's what you're looking for, you won't find it here. That wasn't just some one-night stand. I was in a relationship with that man."

"A relationship with Miller McCall?" he asked, looking surprised.

"You know him?"

"Knew him. He's dead."

Kate gripped the slick stair railing. She'd suspected that he was dead but hadn't known for sure. Not until now. She should feel something. Sadness, or regret, perhaps, but she didn't feel anything but shameful relief.

Dalton watched her face, and as if he could read her every thought, he said, "He won't hurt you ever again."

A wave of anger washed through her. "You don't know me. He didn't hurt me."

"I can hear a lie."

He shouldn't do that. He shouldn't hint that he was more than human. He shouldn't have shown his strength like that in the yard either. He was going to make it impossible for her to hide that she knew what he was.

"You can sleep on my couch for one night. I have a big knife under my pillow."

"Noted," he said, standing too smoothly, as if he hadn't even stiffened up in the cold. He wasn't a careful werewolf. He should be more cautious. People in town were already suspicious. The McCalls didn't hide well enough. They just got angry if someone figured them out. Miller hurt people who got too close to the truth.

"One night, and you have to get out of here when I leave for work in the morning."

"Will do," he said as he jogged down the slick steps with the balance of a mountain goat.

"And if you steal anything from me, I'll call the police."

"I'm not a McCall," he said darkly as he shrugged out of his jacket.

She'd noticed in the bar how well-built he was in a gray sweater that clung to his defined chest like a second skin. That was part of the reason she'd been so mortified he'd been watching her video. He was intimidatingly handsome, and he'd been looking at her naked body, listening to her— oh, gosh.

"I have an extra toothbrush," she blurted out to stop her descent into embarrassment again. "Not because I have people over like this, but because I just bought a new one for myself. It's purple with sparkles."

"That'll do." He strode into her small bathroom like he knew his way around the apartment, and while he was in there, she rushed around and tidied up her small apartment. Mr. Harris used most of the storage off the main room, so things tended to get cluttered in her living space.

Kate smoothed her messy bun before she spread the red blanket over the couch and pulled a pillow off her bed in the corner, then put that onto his make-shift sleeping place, too.

Dalton didn't miss a beat when he came out of the restroom. He took one look at the couch, then lifted the pillow to his nose. "Smells like you. Honey."

She smelled like honey? "I eat it on my oatmeal in the mornings."

Dalton didn't respond, only kicked out of his boots and peeled off his sweater. Her eyes nearly bugged out of her head, and she couldn't pull her gaze away from his muscular back if she tried. Partly, she was attracted to his smooth skin and rippling muscles as he moved, but also, she was hypnotized by the massive tattoo. It was a black ink rendering of a masculine phoenix that snaked this way and that across his back. It looked fearsome, mid-scream, talons outstretched, dots and drips of ink around it as if the bird had been painted on his back like a messy watercolor on paper. The thick, black flaming tail feathers ended just above his low slung jeans.

Her fingers itched to touch it. To trace the harsh lines and brush her fingertips down the etched feathers. It was beautiful and terrifying and sexy all at once.

Dalton froze, his pants mid-zip in his hands. Slowly, he turned and looked at her over his shoulder.

"I like your tattoo," she said on a breath. Scrunching up her face, she murmured, "Sorry. I should give you privacy."

She busied herself with turning off the light, and then she carefully made her way around the coffee table to her bed.

"I got the tattoo a couple years ago," Dalton said in the dark.

"What does it mean?"

"Lots of things." He went quiet, and the sound of fabric rustling filled the air, as if he were getting more comfortable on the couch.

With a sigh, Kate pulled the comforter up to her chin and rolled onto her side, facing him. She couldn't see worth crap in the dark, but giving a werewolf her back just didn't feel right.

"I lost someone," he murmured. "Two someones. The tattoo was a way to focus on coming out of it."

"Rising from the ashes like a phoenix."

"Yeah. Something like that."

His admission he'd lost someone hit her hard, right in the middle. She curled around the pain. She hadn't lost anyone to death yet. Miller had been in and out of her life like a bitterly cold wind. He didn't count. But she'd lost people in her life to other stuff. Betrayal was a big one, and for a couple of them, it felt like they'd died instead of just exited her life.

In an attempt at levity, she admitted, "I have a tattoo, too."

"Yeah?" Dalton sounded interested, and the covers rustled again.

She squinted in the dark, and it looked like he was sitting up on the couch now.

"It's little."

"What is it?"

"An evergreen tree."

"Where?"

"On my ribcage."

More rustling, and now he was lying down again. "Sounds hot."

She laughed. "Oh yes, that's me," she muttered sarcastically. "I've always been known as the hot one."

"Okay, what were you known as then?"

"The responsible one." And the one time she hadn't been, she'd fallen for an undeserving werewolf. Determined not to let her mind or this conversation wander there, she said, "Goodnight."

There was a beat of silence before Dalton murmured, "'Night."

As she stared at the dark lump on the couch, she was appalled at herself all over again because she'd thought she learned her lesson after Miller, but here she was with a man just as dangerous.

And because of her broken instincts, stupidly, she felt safe.

She would probably never get to sleep.

THREE

A scratching sound woke Kate from the deep, dark folds of slumber. Holy moly, it was hard to force her eyes open. Had she been drugged at the bar last night? No, she hadn't even had a drink. She'd only bought a flask of whiskey and then...Dalton!

Kate sat up in bed. Somehow, she was on the very edge, and when she looked in horror at the other side of the bed, it was rumpled and the pillow dented, as if someone had been lying beside her.

Dalton sat on the couch with a cup of steaming coffee he'd apparently made from her coffee maker. He had been in the middle of scribbling something onto a piece of computer paper, but now sat frozen, staring at her.

"Good morning," he said with a smirk.

"Did we..." She looked pointedly at the rumpled side of the bed. "Did we...you know?"

"Sleep together?"

With a gulp, she nodded.

"Your hair looks awesome in the mornings. Like a lion's mane. Fierce and messy and—"

"Did we sleep together?"

"You don't remember asking me to sleep beside you?"

"No," she whispered, shaking her head in denial.

"You definitely did. I told you 'no,' but you tried to shove yourself onto this tiny-ass couch with me. We didn't fit."

"You cuss a lot."

"You don't cuss enough," he countered, one dark eyebrow jacked up in a challenge.

"I don't remember any of that. But...admittedly, I also don't remember sleeping that soundly in...well...a couple years. What are you writing?"

"Nothing," he said with a frown at the paper he was crumpling up in his hands.

"Let me see it."

"It was just a goodbye note. Doesn't matter. Now I can tell you goodbye myself. So, goodbye." He stood, abandoning his coffee.

He couldn't leave! Not after last night. Not like this. She didn't know his number, or where he lived. "I have to get another night's sleep like that!" she blurted out, tripping over the crumpled comforter that had ensnared her legs like an anaconda. With a yelp, she went down hard, nostrils first. But just before she hit the ground, Dalton was there, yanking her up from a painful fate.

"Dammit, Kate, wait until your legs are working, woman."

"You blurred." Shoot, she hadn't meant to say that. "You're fast. Really fast. Were you in track in high school?" *Good cover, now laugh at your joke.* She let off an insane giggle as he stared down at her like she'd lost her mind. This was going awesome. "Can you spend the night tonight?" She groaned and clamped her hands over her mouth.

Dalton released his grip on her shoulders and patted her wild hair carefully, his face stoic. "I don't think that's a good idea."

"Why not?"

"Because you snore like a freight train."

An offended sound worked its way up her throat. "I do not."

"No, you don't," he admitted through a grin.

"It's just…" She took a steadying breath and blinked her eyes slowly, making them nice and round like her sister did when she wanted to get her way. Dalton didn't look impressed so she stopped with the owl eyes and crossed her arms over her chest. Double shoot, she definitely wasn't wearing a bra. Clearing her throat primly, she muttered, "I don't sleep well."

"I have my own cabin to sleep at while I'm in town, Kate, and trust me when I say, it's safer for both of us if we say goodbye here and forget about each other."

There was warning in his voice, so she dared a glance up at his face, then back down his taut chest and flexing abs. Her thoughts muddied.

"Kate."

"Hmmm?"

"To have a conversation, you have to actually respond."

She crossed her arms tighter over her free-jiggling boobs. "Well then put on a darned shirt."

Dalton snorted and shook his head as he turned for his sweater that was draped over the back of the old ladder-back chair by the front door. "I don't know why me not having a shirt on bothers you now. You were petting me like a housecat all damned night."

"Language!"

"You language! The word *darned* offends me." His eyes sparked with amusement when he glanced back at her angry face, the oaf.

"I was not petting you. Right?" She stared at the rumpled comforter on the bed, trying to remember, but all she could recall was blissful sleep. She should sniff his pillow. It probably smelled like him. Yummy.

"You definitely were petting me, and it was hard to sleep."

"Men like petting."

"Men don't like lying there trying to be good and respectful with a raging boner, lady."

She gasped. "Dalton!"

"Look," he muttered, pulling his sweater down to cover his abs. "I'm not good for you or anyone else. A man like me doesn't pair up well."

"I'm not asking you to pair up with me, just sleep with me! No, that's not what I mean. Just sleep *with* me. You know. Beside me? As two separate beings, just sleeping. Together. In the same general vicinity. On the same bed. Or in the same apartment, which ever works best for you."

He had hooked his hands on his hips and stared at her as she fumbled along. "I'm sorry about your sleeping problems but—"

"I'll pay you! I'll hire you. You're like this security blanket, and I know it sounds stupid but I'm desperate for sleep. I can't even remember the last time I hit REM, and I work a stressful job at the medical center and I've been walking around in a haze for the last two years, hoping for a few hours of chopped-up sleep a night. I feel safe with you."

Dalton looked shocked for the span of two breaths before he scanned her tiny apartment pointedly. "Lady, your instincts are broken. And even if they weren't, I have a job. I don't need your money and, anyway, I'm not going to be in Galena for long."

Her acute disappointment was so heavy she dropped her arms and slumped her shoulders. Trying not to pout too obviously, she sat on the edge of the mattress and sighed. "When do you leave?"

"When I want. My boss gives me this time of year off."

"Why?" she asked, frowning up at him.

Dalton shifted his weight and stared off into the kitchen as seconds of silence ticked by. "Because of my losses."

She straightened her spine. "Is it the anniversary?"

He still wouldn't look at her, but he dipped his chin once.

Oh, she felt like dirt. Less than dirt. She felt like the bacteria on the dirt that earthworms ate and then pooped out. Here she was begging for him to alleviate her insomnia problems, and he was clearly dealing with something incredibly painful of his own. "I'm sorry."

Dalton arched his dark, sexy gaze to her. "You're a nurse, right?"

"Yes." Her voice cracked on the word, so she cleared her throat and said it stronger. "Yes, I am."

"Then you can afford a place bigger than this, right?"

She crossed her arms again and tried to glare, but couldn't hold his gaze. His eyes were lightening by the second and were now the color of milk chocolate instead of dark. "I could, but Mr. Harris is my landlord, and he's really nice. My rent money has him so close to paying off his mortgage, and besides, I'm saving up."

"To float the entire town with your good deeds?"

"No." Rude. "For a cabin of my own. I want land and a place outside of town."

Dalton looked shocked. "You're going to be a homesteader?"

"What? No! I just want land for…stuff."

"What kind of stuff?"

"Geez, you're nosy."

"Not nosey. Just curious."

"I like dogs."

Dalton's face hardened in an instant. "What do you mean?"

"I mean," she rushed out, "I want to breed sled dogs for the Iditarod someday. I love nursing, but Galena is population five hundred, and most days at the medical center are really slow. I get several days off in a row each week, and I want to manage and sell sled dogs as a hobby, then eventually full time. It's what my parents did before they moved to Anchorage and retired. My sister and her husband do the same over near Kaltag, right off the Yukon. My family has a reputation for good dogs."

Dalton reared back as recognition flickered across his face. "Hawke Huskies?"

"Yes."

"Wow." He actually looked impressed. "And you turned out to be a nurse? You're a complicated woman, Kate."

"Not complicated, just the responsible one, remember? Getting a successful dog breeding business off the ground isn't easy, family name or no."

"I'd argue nursing isn't easy either."

She gave a surprised laugh. "You'd be right."

When she dropped her gaze from his striking face, she got all caught up on his erection, pressing against the front of his jeans. Dalton followed her look down and frowned. "I should go." He turned and pulled his jacket off the arm of the couch, then pulled it on and zipped it up. He was really going to leave.

She swallowed down the urge to throw a ridiculous amount of money at him if he would only sleep here a few hours a night. Clearly, he had enough going on with his personal life without her complicating his sleeping arrangements. Still, she didn't want him to go. She wanted to learn more about him. She even wanted to know more about why he was different from Miller and his brothers. Why Dalton was nice and protective where the McCalls had been harsh and out of control. She wanted to know where he lived, and why he was leaving so soon, where he worked, and how he'd learned to fight like he'd done with Darren. She wanted to know why he'd given in and slept beside her last night. And most importantly, she wanted to know why she felt so safe around him.

All these questions built up in her throat until she couldn't do more than make a little questioning whimper as he opened the front door, allowing the frigid, late season breeze to swirl around her little apartment.

"What about your coffee?" she asked in desperation as he topped the stairs above her.

"You can have it." He turned and cast her a thoughtful look. She would give her femur bone to know what he was thinking right now with his eyes blazing like they were. "Don't engage with Darren anymore."

"Are you worried?" *Then perhaps you should spend nights with me!*

"You're not mine to worry over, Kate," he said so quietly she almost didn't hear him over the early morning wind.

Without another word, he turned and walked away, his boots crunching in the snowy yard until she couldn't see or hear him anymore.

The ease with which he left her was telling enough. She might have all these questions about him, but he had no interest in her.

You're not mine to worry over. For some reason those words hurt more than was reasonable.

He was a complete stranger, and she wasn't his problem.

FOUR

Dalton watched Kate lock her basement door and make her way up the stairs and through the front yard to her four-wheeler, coffee thermos in her hand. She wore a heavy jacket and pink ear-muffs to match her petal-pink scarf. White rimmed sunglasses hid her eyes. She looked so fucking cute with her tight little scrubs hugging her sexy curves as she ripped the engine of her ATV.

Kate passed right by the street he was parked on, but she didn't look up from the icy road in front of her.

Go get her.

Dalton growled a warning to his wolf to shut up. He scrubbed his hand down his face and resisted the urge to follow her. He would not hunt her like some McCall. Clearly Miller had already done that.

She was that asshole's perfect target—kind, overly-caring, and submissive with a generous heart. Miller had used up women like her when he was alive. Dalton had seen it personally on the few occasions he'd visited a town at the same time as Miller. Dalton had hated him and Cole McCall both.

Miller complicated things, even from the grave. He was Link's late brother, and here Dalton was, unable to pull his gaze away from one of Miller's ex-girlfriends…or whatever she'd been to him.

A long snarl rattled his throat just thinking about Miller fucking her in that stupid video.

Gritting his teeth, he shook his head at what he was about to do. A wise werewolf didn't catch the attention of a ruthless enforcer like Clayton, much less ask favors. Right now, though, he was helpless to leave her like this. He had to do something to make her life a little better. He'd be a shit mate for her, but he could do this.

Dalton hovered his finger over the damning number for a moment before he jammed it down and waited for Clayton to pick up.

"Dalton," the enforcer greeted. What the hell? He'd never talked to him on the phone, so how had Clayton even recognized this number?

"I have a favor to ask."

"Of course you do," Clayton said dryly.

"It's not for me. It's for a woman Miller McCall hurt."

Silence grew thick as fog over the line. "Did he kill her?"

"No, but he posted a video that is shaming her. Tagged her name to it and everything. Do you have any connections for someone who could take that offline?"

"My focus is more on enforcement and the McCall cure."

Dalton gritted his teeth and adjusted his position on the cold seat of his snow machine. "So is that a no?"

"I'm not some fairy godfather, Dalton. I have no interest in granting wishes for nothing."

Dalton spat in the snow and barely resisted a dark laugh. "I'll owe you one."

Clayton sighed into the phone. "Who is she to you?"

The one.

Dalton swallowed his wolf's words down. He'd said that before, and he'd been wrong. "She's a nice lady who doesn't deserve what Miller did to her."

"Hmmm," Clayton said noncommittally. "What's her name?"

"Katherine Hawke. Miller did something to her. Broke something. She can't sleep after him." Shit. He shook his head at the memory of Kate screaming out in her sleep last

50

night. Of how he'd held her tight until she'd settled against his chest. She hadn't asked for him to sleep beside her. That had been his first lie to her. Dalton hadn't been able to help himself when her nightmare had started. And already, his wolf would die just to ease her pain if he could.

With Clayton, Dalton was giving too much away and forgetting who the Silvers' father really was. He wasn't a friend. He was a dangerous grizzly shifter with the power to give kill orders on a whim.

"I'll get it taken care of," Clayton said low. "Give me a day. You owe me."

The line clicked, and when Dalton drew his cell in front of his face, the call had ended and the screen blank. Nice.

With a growl, Dalton shoved the phone in his back pocket. He had to get out of here. His April First spiral had to be over early this year because it was dangerous to stay in town. Here in Galena, he was too close to Link and that beautiful baby girl of his. He was too close to the family who reminded him the most of what he'd lost. But that wasn't the only reason why he would have to leave town first thing in the morning.

The meat of the matter was that his interest in Kate was dangerous for them both.

His wolf was marking his territory with every moment he sat in front of her apartment and laying claim to a woman he had no shot in hell at keeping happy.

Whatever had happened with Miller had brought her to her knees, and Dalton didn't want to be the weight that pinned her to the ground. He was a wildfire, burning everything good in his life to ashes. Only shifters survived him—Chance, Link, the Silvers.

Dalton was a realist, and the cold, hard fact was he'd given his first mate all he had—everything he was—and still, he'd fallen miles short.

Kate was a good person. Maybe she was the most selfless person he'd ever met.

And she definitely deserved better than him.

FIVE

Dalton pulled his snow machine through the last line of piney woods before the clearing that housed Link's old cabin. His alpha was still making payments on the place, but for the life of him, Dalton couldn't figure out why. Last year, Link had moved into Nicole's cabin on the next property over, and now this cabin sat vacant except on the rare occasions he and Chance made their way to Galena. Not that he was complaining. This place sure beat the hell out of staying at some bed and breakfast in town. His wolf liked to roam the land here. In a way, it felt like a second home to Dalton, right under the temporary room he lived in at Silver Summit Outfitters where he worked as an outdoor guide.

Dalton narrowed his eyes at the figure sitting on the front porch stairs. Chance Dawson, his cousin and the final leg of their pack, was waiting for him with an overnight bag sitting on the snowy porch beside him. Freaking great. Just what he needed.

Angry enough to spit nails, Dalton skidded to a stop and cut the engine. "Please tell me you're not here to intervention me."

"I'm not here to intervention you," Chance said blandly. The douche-wagon didn't even try to hide the lie.

A snarl ripped through Dalton as he climbed the porch stairs two at a time and blasted past his cousin and into the house. Chance followed him in and set his overnight bag just inside the door.

"Nuh uh," Dalton said, pacing the kitchen. "There's a cabin out back for you. This ain't a slumber party."

"That's a shed."

"It has log walls, a furnace, and a bed. It's a damned cabin."

Chance's gaze drifted to the picture frame on the coffee table. Gritting his teeth against a string of curses at being busted, Dalton slammed the picture face down. "One week, Chance. I asked for one week alone. It hasn't changed in four years, yet here you are, breaking my one damned request for the fourth year in a row. Why can't you let me have it? I just want one week to get out of my head."

"You done?" Chance asked, sinking into the couch cushion and lifting his boot onto the coffee table. He came dangerously close to hitting the picture frame.

Dalton cracked his knuckles as he paced. "I'm going back tomorrow."

"Why?"

Because I met someone who scares the shit out of me. "Because I'm tired of being here."

Chance narrowed his eyes to bright green slits, and his blond brows drew down suspiciously. He leaned forward and rested his elbows on his knees as he studied Dalton in silence. "What's going on? Where were you last night?"

Dalton scrubbed his hands roughly through his hair, then busied himself with stripping off his winter layers. When Chance only watched him in that uncanny, annoying, knowing way of his, Dalton admitted, "I was with a woman."

"Like fucking a woman?"

"No." Dalton swallowed hard. The last thing he needed right now was Chance giving him shit over a crush. There was no escaping this conversation, though. Chance wasn't like Link, who didn't know how hard and how long to push. Dalton and Chance had grown up together, and his cousin knew that all he had to do was wait and Dalton, like an idiot, would spill his guts eventually.

Letting off a short growl, he sank into the single chair across from the couch. Glaring at Chance, he muttered, "I didn't fuck her. I just slept beside her."

Chance's brows rose so high they made wrinkles on his forehead. Huffing a surprised sound, as if he'd been punched in the gut, Chance relaxed back into the couch cushions. "Did you spoon?"

"See, I knew you'd give me shit—"

"I'm not making fun of you, man. It's a serious question. Did. You. Spoon?"

After a few drawn-out seconds to make sure Chance was being serious, he answered, "Mostly I hugged her to my chest. I was supposed to sleep on the couch, but she had a nightmare and I…I don't know…calmed her down."

"And how did that feel?"

"Are you a therapist now? What do you mean how did it feel? It felt awesome. She wasn't repulsed, she didn't flinch away, she pet me in her sleep like I was her favorite parakeet, and when we woke up in the morning, she wasn't disgusted with the fact that she'd slept beside me. There was no guilt. She looked at me like I was normal, and she told me I make her feel safe. So, yeah. It felt nice."

"You make her feel safe?" Chance's lips stretched in a slow smile. "Well, that's a new one."

Dalton sighed. "Yeah, well I didn't say it made any sense. I just said it felt nice. I heard you told Link about April First, you dick."

Chance shrugged one shoulder unapologetically. "At some point, he should know. He's our alpha."

"Out of convenience."

"Bullshit. Link is doing a better job than we thought he could. He's doing better than either one of us would do at the head of a pack. You just want to keep everyone at arm's length."

Dalton leaned his elbows on his knees and stared at the wood floors between his boots. "Can you blame me?"

"Nah, I don't blame you. I blame Shelby."

"Don't."

"Think real hard, Dalton. Did Shelby let you cuddle her? Did she let you console her? Did she calm from a panic because you were there? I was there for the aftermath of every hard day with her. I saw Shelby for what she was. You didn't. You still don't."

"She was my mate."

"False. She talked shit about you behind your back whenever she got the chance, and she never allowed you to claim her."

"She didn't know I was a werewolf."

"Why? Why didn't you ever tell her?"

Dalton clenched his jaw as he was pummeled with the hundred reasons why he hid the biggest part of him from a woman he'd loved. "Because she wasn't trustworthy with our secret," he ground out.

"Then how could she be your mate? You didn't give her a claiming mark. You hid yourself away. You let her verbally ream you all the fucking time, and I hated to see it. I hated her. You're a beast, Dalton. You always were, and you let someone make you feel less than. You *let* her. You let her bend you until you almost broke."

"She was the mother of our child."

Chance scratched the blond, three-day beard on his face. His eyes pooled with sympathy but his words didn't match. "*Your* child, Dalton. You and I both know Shelby never wanted that baby." Chance flipped over the picture frame. "Look at her. Look at her eyes. There is no softness there, no kindness. She could barely muster a damned smile for a picture, Dalton. You weren't the unworthy one. She was."

Slowly, Dalton leaned forward and picked up the picture frame. In it, he and Shelby were standing in front of their house in Anchorage. He had his arm draped around her shoulders, and his other hand proudly cradled her round belly. The smile on his face was big, dopey almost. But Shelby's mouth only lifted a little at the corners, and her eyes looked dead. It wasn't the baby that had drained their relationship either. Every picture they took together was like this. She had liked the life he could provide her, but beyond that, she didn't like him touching her. She didn't like holding his hand or kissing him in public. Now that he looked back on it, she hadn't seemed to enjoy kissing him at all. How had he not realized that until now? He'd brought this picture because she'd looked beautiful in it, full with his child, but Chance was right. Her eyes were cold. They always had been, even when she told him she loved him.

Dalton dropped the picture in a rush, desperate not to touch it anymore.

"When you lost Amelia, it ripped my guts out," Chance said in a thick voice. "I know how much you wanted her to be a boy so she could live. I know how much you wanted to be a dad. But you didn't see it there in Shelby's eyes."

Dalton couldn't look Chance in the eye, not when he was riled up and reeling like this. "Didn't see what?"

"The relief on her face."

"Don't say that."

"You couldn't see it, but I was right there, standing in the doorway while she held Amelia's little body, and she wouldn't even look at the baby. She just stared out the window with this relieved look like she'd dodged a bullet, man. She wasn't the mate for you, and she sure as fuck wasn't the right mother for your child. You said it yourself. She. Wasn't. Trustworthy."

"Why didn't you tell me all of this before?"

"I tried, but you weren't ready."

"But I'm ready now?" Dalton had tried and failed to hide the disgust from his voice. All this time, he'd been mourning a breakup with someone who hadn't felt the same, who wasn't mourning him back.

I wanted her to love us back.

Stupid wolf had fogged his vision. Dalton shook his head, his thoughts spinning as each memory took on a new meaning. All of the I-hate-yous hadn't been his fault. They'd been hers. Who even used those three words as weapons? He hadn't deserved them as he'd thought. She'd just known how to cut him the deepest.

And he'd let her. Chance was right. He'd opened himself up and allowed it.

"I feel so stupid," he murmured, linking his hands behind his head.

"Nah, you aren't. You would've dealt with it differently if you hadn't lost Amelia. If she'd never been pregnant, you would've left her. You bonded with that little baby in her tummy, not Shelby. It got you all mixed up."

In a flash of anger, Dalton stood and yanked the frame off the table, then strode for the front door and chucked the picture as far into the woods as he could. A part of him felt liberated, but a bigger part of him felt shame for allowing Shelby to taint his April First. That had been the day Amelia had died. Female werewolves hadn't been able to survive before Vera cured Link's little girl. She'd passed at the beginning of April, the day after she was born, and Shelby had ended their relationship then, too.

He'd lost everything he'd ever wanted, everything he'd fought for, in one day.

Chest heaving, he scanned Link's winter white woods as his throat tightened up.

"What's her name?" Chance asked softly from behind him.

"Who?"

"You know who. The one who made you ready to hear what I've been trying to tell you."

"Kate." Dalton rolled his eyes closed and inhaled deeply, imagining the scent of honey. It calmed him little by little until his breath came steady. "Kate Hawke."

SIX

Kate smiled politely at Dr. Vega and waved goodnight. He'd been in a beast of a mood tonight and yelled at her twice for no good reason, but she forgave him. His brother had been sick for a long time, and he was open with his worry for his family, but Dr. Vega tended to take out his frustrations on the clinic staff when he was at work.

He jerked his chin as a goodbye and lowered his attention back to the paperwork on the nurse station countertop. She didn't wait around for an apology. That man didn't give them. Really, no men gave apologies. They took what they wanted, drained the women around them, then moved on. Or died, apparently.

She shook her head hard to punish thoughts of Miller out of her mind. He had been terrifying in the end of their relationship, or whatever it was they were doing, but in the beginning, he'd pretended to be nice. It was those few days of the pretend caring that had gotten her all jumbled up with the news of his death. She felt guilty for being sad. There. There it was. He deserved to be in the ground, but she was still sad at the loss of a life she'd known once.

The snow was falling in thick sheets, and she high-kneed it through the deepest parts on the way to an awning that protected her four-wheeler from the Alaskan weather. There were a couple of other ATVs sitting under there with hers. She owned a truck, but it liked to fishtail in weather like this, so on the snowiest days, she used her little off-roader to make her way through town. It wasn't like Galena was huge. The only reason they could afford a police station and medical center was because this was prime real estate right off the Yukon where boaters were frequent in the warm months. This was the place where all the tiny towns in the surrounding area could load up on supplies. There were a couple of bush pilots who lived here that kept this place stocked as long as the weather was flyable.

She loved it here. Or she had before Miller. Before the video that kept her in shame. Everyone in this town had probably seen it. Oh sure, she kept her head up, but the whispers of a small town were hard even on the toughest souls, and she was quite meek.

A black Chevy truck with fat tires and chains on the wheels came to a stop behind her, blocking her from backing out. In an instant, fear pummeled her heart. Was it Darren, back to finish what he'd started? But the truck was older, and not the right model.

When the window rolled down, she froze. Dalton's eyes danced, but for a few moments, neither one of them said anything, only stared at each other until she offered him a shy smile. "I thought I would never see you again."

"That was the plan."

She wiped a thin layer of snow off the taillights of her ATV just for something to do other than swim in his too-handsome gaze. "What are you doing here?"

Dalton relaxed back into his seat, arm draped over the wheel as he dragged his attention out the front window. "I'm going to be shitty at this."

"At what?"

His jaw clenched, but when he looked at her again, a smile lingered right at the corners of his lips. "I'll take the job."

"The job?"

He lifted his chin and waited, cocky, sexy man.

"Oh, you want to sleep with me."

His smile deepened, and her heart banged against her chest. Dalton was the most striking man she'd ever seen, and he was here, talking to her.

"We should negotiate terms over dinner."

"Dinner?" Was he asking her out? On a date?

She swallowed down her immediate, high-pitched answer just so she wouldn't look too eager. "It's late. Not much is open at midnight around here."

"Yeah, when I planned this, I didn't know you worked so late."

"My schedule changes all the time, depending on when I'm needed. Uuum," she said, desperately thinking of somewhere they could go because she definitely wanted to go on a date with Dalton, even if it was the middle of the night. "There's the Taco Trailer. It stays open late. It's right beside the bar so when last call ends, the heavy drinkers can eat and sober up a bit before they go home."

"Perfect." He looked at her ATV. "You know how to load that thing?"

"Oh, I can just meet you there."

"I don't like you cold."

"Oh. Okay. Yeah, I can load it. Do you have a ramp?"

Dalton shoved his door open and disappeared around the other side of the truck, then lowered the tailgate and pulled out a couple of long metal pieces with grooves. He set them at a comfortable angle, then leaned on the side of his truck, arms crossed as he waited. He wore a white sweater that clung to the muscular curves of his arms, but no jacket. He didn't even look cold, but maybe that was a werewolf thing. She didn't know for sure, nor would she ask because she still had to be careful not to let on that she'd guessed what he really was. She might like him a ridiculous amount, but she'd liked Miller at first, too, and he'd turned poisonous.

"I'd offer to load it, but I have a feeling you can take care of yourself just fine."

That drew her up short. "Why do you say that?"

"Am I wrong?"

"No," she said softly, struggling to hold his direct gaze. "I can take care of myself, but usually people underestimate me. They always do, actually." Before he could respond to that mortifying bit of personal information she'd just shared, she turned and hopped over the seat of the four-wheeler, then started the engine. Backing through her exhaust fumes, she pulled a wide loop in the parking lot and lined it up, then hit the throttle and drove it carefully up the ramp and into the back of Dalton's truck. Without a word, he began to wench straps onto it to secure the ATV in place as she climbed down one of the jacked-up tires and onto the snowy ground.

"Go on, get warm inside. I'll finish up here."

She stood there for a moment, a few feet away from where he worked, unable to look up from the ground with the silly thought that had just gone through her head. She'd missed him. Really missed him. Especially when she'd thought she wouldn't ever see him again.

Closing her eyes so she wouldn't see the rejection, she took a giant step forward and wrapped her arms around his waist. He went rigid, so she whispered, "Hi."

Dalton let off a long sigh and relaxed under her hug. Slowly, he slid his arms around her shoulders, then shocked her silly when he rested his cheek against the top of her head. "Hi," he murmured in that deep, sexy timbre of his.

God, he smelled good. That same feeling of safety washed over her, making her feel two-shot tequila drunk.

"You're shaking," he said above the sound of his idling truck. "Go on, get in. I really don't want you cold. It makes me…"

"Makes you what?"

Dalton shook his head and eased back, only inches from her face. His smile had disappeared, and his eyes were that blazing caramel color again. She should be scared, but she couldn't muster any fear.

"It makes me want to take care of you."

She let off a long, shaky breath. Oooh, she liked him. "I'm not shaking from the cold. I'm shaking because you make me the good kind of nervous." Her stomach was currently doing flip-flops just being this close to him.

He searched her eyes, then dipped his too-bright gaze to her lips.

Please kiss me.

Smoothly, he eased her backward, step-by-step until her back pressed against the side of his truck. He cupped her neck and lowered his lips toward hers. But just an inch away, he hesitated. "Kate," he whispered, a slight frown marring his handsome face. "I should leave you alone."

That's not what she wanted, though. She didn't want him to leave at all. Pushing up slightly, she pressed her lips against his and reveled in the way he softened for her. Soft kiss, rough scratch of his short stubble. Such a sexy contrast. Dalton angled his head and moved against her, sipping her mouth until he'd built a fire in her middle. She gripped onto his sweater and pulled his waist closer to feel more of his body heat. Dalton drew her bottom lip between his teeth and bit it gently between kisses, and now she was four-shot tequila drunk. And when he pressed his hips forward, she could feel it. He was aroused, and it was because of her. She'd done that. She was turning on a man like Dalton

Dawson, and a layer of insecurity slipped away like the exhaust from the back of his truck.

Dalton's tongue brushed her lip, and she opened automatically for him, eyes tightly closed to fully melt into this moment. She'd never been kissed like this. She'd never felt like this.

He sunk his tongue into her mouth, and a helpless, needy moan wrenched up her throat. Dalton answered with a soft, sexy growl. He ended the kiss with a quiet smack, then rested his forehead on hers as his chest heaved.

"Sorry," he murmured, hands slipping from her neck to her waist.

She laughed and blinked hard once, trying to clear her tipsy thoughts. "You should definitely not apologize for kissing me like that, mister."

Dalton chuckled, but he was hiding his eyes now, veiling the color by looking at the ground beside them.

With a frown, Kate cupped his cheeks and tried to bring him back, but he wasn't having it. He kissed the palm of her glove instead and eased away, then busied himself with shutting the tail gate.

"Kate, please. Warm." His voice sounded strange now. Too deep, too gravelly.

She wished she could tell him she understood why he was pulling away. She wished she could tell him she knew about the animal, and that it was okay, but if he didn't want to share that part with her, she had to accept that. Miller had hidden it for the six months they'd dated. Maybe it was werewolf law, or maybe Dalton didn't trust her. Either way, he didn't want to let her in. It stung, but this wasn't about her. Hiding was his choice.

Pain burned through her chest, as if he'd dragged a hot poker underneath her sternum. To hide the hurt from his rejection after the most incredible kiss of her life, she pulled open the door to his truck and climbed inside while he finished strapping the ATV in the back.

When he climbed behind the wheel, his eyes were as dark as night again. She was already thawing out, but he turned up the heat anyway as she stared out the window.

"What's wrong?" he asked.

"Nothing."

"I'm sorry I kissed you."

"Shhh!" She clenched her hands in her lap to stop the urge to punch him in the arm.

Dalton gripped the wheel in a choke hold. "Did you just shhh me?"

"Yes."

"Why?"

She crossed her arms over her chest as the tips of her ears turned hot. "I don't want to talk about it."

"Woman, I don't get hints, and I can't read your mind. Tell me what I did wrong and be done with it. I want tacos."

She wasn't confrontational, and she liked to think she was too smart to start an argument in the cab of a pickup with a freaking werewolf, but he'd seriously just slammed on the brakes and then apologized for kissing her like he regretted it.

"Kate!"

"If you regret kissing me so much, I don't really want to get tacos with you anymore. I'm tired and have to work again tomorrow."

"I thought you needed me to apologize! Women like that shit!"

Kate reeled back. "What women are you talking about? No woman wants to get the kiss of her life and then have it immediately taken back, Dalton."

He scrubbed his hands over his face and relaxed back on the headrest. "I told you I would be shitty at this. I don't know jack about girls or making them happy. It would be best for both of us if—"

"Don't you freaking finish that sentence, Dalton Dawson. Save your break-up-before-we-begin speech for someone who wants it." She sighed an irritated sound. "Buy me tacos."

He rolled his face toward her, his dark brows drawn down suspiciously.

"I'm serious," she said, daring to show him her blushing cheeks. "I want three. And extra hot sauce."

Dalton's lips lifted in a stunning smile, and he snorted. He threw the truck in drive and eased out of the parking lot. "Did we just have an argument?"

"Yes, and I hated it."

"I don't regret the kiss, you know. It was kind of amazing. I just…"

"Freaked out?"

"Yeah."

"I had a man who was only half in with me before. I'm not looking for that again."

"Miller?"

"Him and my first ex. I want to be a girl a man *chooses*, you know? I don't want to just be a safe decision because a man is afraid of being alone."

With one hand, Dalton turned the wheel onto the main drag in Galena. "Can I ask you a question?"

"Sure."

"Why Miller?"

Kate scrunched up her nose. "How well did you know him?"

"Well enough to know he was a grade-A mega-chode."

"Yeah, well, I didn't figure that out until month three of our relationship. He was nice to me at first, and he was a bit of a bad-boy. I was spiraling after a rough break-up, and he took the edge off my loneliness for a while. It was fun to make a risky decision for once in my life."

"And what happened?"

Kate ghosted a glance at his profile, then fiddled with a loose string on her gloves. How stupid was it to admit she'd been so naïve with Miller? After all, she wanted Dalton to actually like her and stay interested.

"You don't have to talk about it. I totally get it. You don't know me, and you don't owe me any explanations." There it was, the out. Dalton was offering her a way to stay hidden, just like him.

She balked. "He posted the video, and when I confronted him about it, he showed no remorse. I was horrified. My mom and dad called because they'd found out about it. They were so deeply disappointed, and my sister left all these awful messages about me ruining our family's reputation. Anyway, Miller got real mean after that."

"Why didn't you break it off with him?"

"I did. He didn't take no for an answer. He kept coming over. Showing up late at night. Scaring me. He kicked in my door during one of my shifts and was waiting for me when I got home."

"Did you call the police?"

"Of course. They'd seen the video, though, and didn't do anything about our little lover's spat. One of the officers said it wasn't right that I was raising red flags on a man when I was obviously a willing party in that tape."

"Shit." Dalton sounded disgusted. He pulled into an iced-over parking spot near the Taco Trailer. "Did he hurt you?"

"Once. He choked me, and I thought I was going to die. He looked insane, but he doubled over on himself and dropped me, then ran out the back door." Into the snow where she'd watched him change into a gray wolf just on the edge of the back porch light. His contorted body and white eyes still visited her nightmares. "Dalton?"

"Hmm?" he asked, more growl than question.

"How did he die?"

Dalton inhaled deeply. "He hurt a woman, cut her face with an ax and went after her man." He slid an unsympathetic look to Kate. "The woman hurt him back."

"Good for her," she murmured. The blinking neon lights cast Dalton's face in greens and blues. She liked Dalton's wolf eyes much more than Miller's. They weren't crazy, just enthralling. "Since we're full speed ahead on this mortification train, do you want to see what I got in the mail the other day?"

Dalton held out his hand. "Yep."

She giggled and pulled out the ripped envelope from her purse, slid the wedding invite out of the thick covering, then set it gingerly onto his palm.

"Dalton read it in the glowing lights of the Taco Trailer. "Whose wedding?"

"My pre-Miller ex."

Dalton slid her a grossed-out look. "Why would he invite you to his wedding?"

"Because Nadine Bertrand," she explained, pointing to the bride's name on the invite, "was my best friend for more than twenty years. Basically since we were fetuses."

Dalton's eyes went wide. "Your ex is marrying your best friend?"

"*Ex* best friend."

"Please tell me they started dating after you broke up."

She stifled a laugh at his expression. "Nope."

"That's fucked up. Wait, you're not going, are you?"

"Heck no. I haven't talked to either of them since I found out. Nadine keeps calling me though, wanting to be friends again. Apparently, she misses me. As you can see, I don't have the best taste in…people."

Dalton huffed a dark laugh. "No, you don't. Wait there," he said, shoving his door open.

"Why? I'm hungry."

"Because, you impatient woman, I'm going to open your door for you."

"I knew this was a date," she murmured, feeling giddy.

Dalton gave her a heart-stopping grin before he closed his door and jogged around to her side. He helped her out of the high cab and settled his hand on her lower back as they approached the food truck. Bats flapped around her stomach as his touch lingered at the base of her spine. How could a man pull such a potent reaction from her body with nothing more than the brush of his palm?

Giddy and a little off-balance, she took a spot in line behind a couple of slurring bar patrons ordering what sounded like one of everything.

After Dalton put their order in and collected their paper-lined baskets of tacos, she sat down at one of the tables right beside the giant heater. It was warm on her back, and she offered Dalton a shy smile as he took a seat right beside her rather than across the table.

At the first bite of steaming taco, she rolled her eyes closed and groaned in ecstasy. It had been a long shift under Dr. Vega, and she hadn't eaten since this morning. "This is my favorite food," she said around a mouthful. "What's your favorite food?"

"Pussy," Dalton said through a baiting grin.

She nearly choked on corn tortilla. "Dalton," she admonished.

He was laughing now as he poured hot sauce over his own tacos. "Meat. I like any kind of meat. The rarer the better."

Another tongue-in-cheek werewolf admission, and now he was looking at her, daring her to ask questions.

"Favorite color?"

The smile fell from Dalton's face. "It used to be blue, but now it's green."

Huh. Her eyes were green. She ducked out of his serious gaze so he wouldn't see the color in her cheeks. "I like your truck."

"Thanks, I just bought it today."

"You did?"

"I borrow my alph—" Dalton shook his head hard and let off a bitter laugh. "I use my friend's snow machine when I visit, but I figured I'd go ahead and get my own ride. I don't have a truck up where I work near Kodiak."

"Do you visit Galena often?"

"Not as often as I should."

"Who is your friend? I bet I'll know him. Everyone knows everyone around here."

Wariness slashed through Dalton's dark eyes. "Lincoln McCall."

Kate squeezed her tortilla so hard the meat plopped out and onto the table. "Lincoln McCall is your friend?" she asked in a choked whisper.

Dalton dipped his chin once in affirmation. He looked like he wanted to say more, but he gritted his teeth and took another bite of food instead. She hadn't missed the slip-up, though. Alph? She'd bet her tits Lincoln McCall, Miller's brother, was his alpha. She knew about wolves. She knew about dogs. She'd been raised around them for goodness sake and was well versed in the similar hierarchy of dog sled teams and wolf packs. She had only met Lincoln a few times. He'd been the quiet one, but still, his eyes had glowed just as terrifyingly as his brother's.

The food sat like a tasteless lump in her mouth, and she gulped it down. She wiped her hands slowly with a napkin, stalling. If she spoke too soon, her voice would shake and give away just how scared she was. He was in a pack with a freaking McCall werewolf.

"You're the one who's freaking out now," he said, scanning the filling tables around them.

"I'm not freaking out."

"Well, before you go make a snap judgement, Link isn't anything like his brothers. He isn't anything like any of his family. He's actually a good guy."

"What do you do out near Kodiak?" she asked, desperate to talk about anything else.

Dalton narrowed his eyes like she wasn't fooling anyone with her subject change, but being the smart man that he was, he dropped it. "I'm an outdoor guide at Silver Summit Outfitters."

"Do you guide hunts?"

"Yeah. I'm good at tracking things. We do seasonal hunts depending on when each animal is legal to take, but I do a lot of camping, hiking, and fishing excursions, too. Right now is our slow season, but in the next couple of months, we have a lot of people from the lower forty-eight who have booked us."

"Who is us?"

"My cousin, Chance, and my friend Jenner Silver."

"Hey, I know him! Jenner lives here now. He moved outside of Galena with his wife last year. They live up on Elyse and Ian's homestead."

"You know Elyse?"

"Yeah, I was her nurse when she got clawed by a bear last year and again when she fell on an ax a couple winters ago…" Kate gasped as something clicked firmly into place. "Elyse. She got cut by an ax across her face."

"I think it's time to go," Dalton said, standing with his empty basket. "You finished?"

She was definitely finished. She stared at him so hard, her eyeballs were actually getting cold. "Elyse killed Miller, didn't she?"

Dalton looked around nervously and lowered down, arm locked on the table. Voice full of warning, he murmured, "Kate, stop. Stop picking at this one."

"But—"

Dalton spun and disappeared around the Taco Trailer. A moment later, he strode off for his truck, hands empty of the baskets. The door slammed, and he floored it out of the parking spot, only to hit the brakes and slide to a stop an instant later.

Through the front window, Dalton lifted his light gaze to her as he gripped the steering wheel.

This was a man who had trained himself to run. Whatever had happened to make him this way, she didn't know and would likely never find out. She'd done this before and didn't want to feel like this again. Like she couldn't ever really get to know the person she cared about. Like an outsider…always a guest in someone's life, but never a main player.

She swallowed the lump in her throat and dared to hold his gaze as she walked up to his truck, then past it to the tailgate, which she lowered.

"What are you doing?" he asked, by her side too fast. She would've startled, but she'd seen speed like his before.

"I think you have too many secrets, and I think you're a runner. I already told you I've done this before. I want more. I don't want to be afraid that you'll bolt when things get hard." She pulled the ramps from between her ATV's tires, rested them at an angle on the tailgate, climbed up into the truck and over the seat of her ride, and turned it on.

Dalton looked ill as he watched her back it down out of his truck, but he didn't stop her. Instead, he stood there with his hands linked behind his head. As she drove away, she looked back once when the word "shit" echoed down the street. He flung his hands forward, his eyes reflecting strangely in the red glow of her taillights. With Miller, that would've scared her, but with Dalton, it filled her with immense sadness.

His wolf intrigued her, but his wolf had pushed her away.

Regrets, regrets, regrets. Dalton Dawson had been broken, too, and though she hurt for him, he wasn't in the same spot she was. She was finally hopeful and wanted something meaningful with someone she cared about. Dalton had started that change in her, but he wasn't capable of seeing it through. There was tragedy in that.

Dalton was a tornado, and he would sweep her into oblivion if she let him.

SEVEN

He was such an idiot. When Dalton pulled over the last crest of a snowy ridge, his headlights arched over Link's cabin. The lights were on inside, which meant Chance was still awake.

Great.

He cut the engine, got out, and slammed the door. God, why was he like this now? He'd been normal once. Well, as normal as a werewolf could be. But now, every April, he turned into a volatile asshole. Oh, he'd read between the lines of Kate's last words. She'd done it before and wanted more, AKA she deserved better. And yeah, he'd known that, but this was all he had to give right now. One minute he felt confident, like he couldn't wait to see her, and then when he actually talked to her, he ducked and dodged any serious conversation that pulled her too close to his life. Too close to the real him.

And what had she done? She'd shared her mistakes with Miller. She'd shown him that damned wedding invite, which had probably caused her bone-deep pain, and he'd given her nothing in return.

What had he hoped for? That their conversations would stay shallow and never go past flirting?

Dalton paced in front of Link's old cabin, wearing a trail in the snow.

He wanted something real.

But his biggest fear was getting something real, and ruining it.

Dalton squatted down and gripped his head as his wolf pushed to escape his skin. His inner animal was clawing and howling to go back to her.

Say sorry. Shelby loved when it you said sorry.

Shelby? Dalton retched in the snow at the pain in his middle. It should've been a woman like Kate holding his baby. He'd picked wrong, and now he was unfixable because of that decision. It had damaged something inside of him to mourn the loss of Amelia alone.

The door to the cabin opened, but Dalton couldn't pull his gaze from the dead grass that poked up from the trail he'd stomped into the snow. He retched again as he tried desperately to keep his human skin.

Nicole's scent hit his nose, and he swallowed hard, dragging his attention up to the top porch stair where she sat down, wrapped in a blanket with a sad look in her dark eyes.

"Dalton," she whispered, sympathy tainting the sound.

"I missed dinner," he said, feeling like shit.

"It's okay."

"No." He settled in the snow, legs folded beneath him. "It's not. Nothing is okay."

Her eyes rimmed with tears. "Link told me about April First. I didn't know."

"I don't like talking about it."

"Dalton, I've been so hurt that you didn't want to be around us. I was mad at you. Mad that you barely look at Fina. Mad that you won't hold her and bond with her. I thought I was to blame somehow. Like you didn't want to be in a pack with me, which now I know is stupid, and I shouldn't have made it about myself. I just didn't understand."

Dalton stood and climbed the stairs, then sat shoulder to shoulder with her, watching the green northern lights in the distance.

Nicole leaned her head on his arm. "I'm sorry. I can't imagine how painful it must be for you to lose your little girl and then have to be around a baby girl who survived."

Dalton sighed a frozen breath. "I'm kind of messed up right now. The rest of the year, I'm okay. Or at least, I can put on the show, right? But you're catching me when I screw up the most. I like to hide out during April. I hurt less people that way, you know? But now Chance, Link, you, and…"

Nicole eased off his shoulder and offered him a confused look. "And who?"

"And this girl I met. There is a hundred percent chance I will let everyone down right now. It's like I can't think straight. I make the wrong decisions. Everything is cloudy, and I don't have much control over my animal or my moods. I should've done my hiding somewhere more remote, but this year, this place seemed…important."

"This place or your pack?"

Dalton shrugged. "Maybe both. I don't know. I've never been in a pack before. It's always just been me and Chance, and we were never officially a pack, you know? And then Link came along and bound us, and now I don't really know how to navigate anything."

"Link and Chance *love* you."

"Strongly *like* you when you aren't being a twat," Chance corrected from inside.

"And you're very important to me, too," Nicole said without missing a beat. "When you're ready, you can lean on us. I don't know how packs work either, but to me, you feel like family. Everything feels better when you and Chance visit. Link is happier. I'm happier. I don't know how it is for you, but when you and Chance are close, it's like my two brothers are in town."

Dalton looked down at Nicole. Her large birthmark, the color of red wine, was stark on her pale cheek. He understood her need for a makeshift family. Hers hadn't been awesome, and her real dad had died the year before she found out he even existed. She'd come here searching for a place to belong, and instead of him being a positive part of her journey, he'd failed her. He'd failed everyone.

"I'll try harder," he promised.

Nicole sniffed and shook her head. "Do things in your own time, Dalton. I understand your reservations now. Link and I will hold. We'll be here for whatever you want this pack to be."

Dalton wiped off the snowy porch floorboard beside him in an effort to avoid her eyes when he asked nonchalantly, "When you found out what Link was, did you freak out?"

"I nearly shot him," she said.

"What?" he asked.

"Whoa, whoa, whoa, what?" Chance asked from where he suddenly shadowed the open doorway. The eavesdropper came to sit on Dalton's other side.

"Yeah, I figured out what he was before he told me, and I came to this place, guns blazing. I thought he was the wolf who killed my father. Turns out Link was only trying to make up for his family's shortcomings. Cole was actually the one who killed my dad." She slid him a glance, then snuggled more deeply into her blanket. "Dalton, you're allowed by shifter law to tell your mate what you are. Clayton can't give a kill order for exposing the wolf to your woman."

Chance snorted. "He couldn't bring himself to tell the mother of his child. He's not telling this one."

There was challenge in his voice, and Dalton growled. He didn't like being baited. "I haven't known her long enough."

"What do you feel?"

"I *feel* like she's amazing, but complicated, and I can't stop thinking about her." Dalton leaned back on his locked arms and stretched his long legs down the stairs. "I also *feel* like her life would be exponentially better if I figured out a way to leave her alone."

"Why?" Nicole asked.

"Because she's Miller McCall's ex-girlfriend. She's been through enough without falling for another monster."

"Oh, damn," Chance said.

"Damn indeed."

"Does she like you?" Nicole asked softly.

Dalton bit the side of his lip thoughtfully and dragged the heel of his boot over the snowy porch, creating an arc across the wood there. "She says I make her feel safe. She doesn't sleep well, but with me...well...she did."

"Wow," Nicole murmured. She was quiet for a long time before she asked, "Do you want my advice?"

"No," he teased.

She elbowed him as he chuckled. "Feeling safe with Link was a really big deal for me. I don't think you should push her away because of what you think is good for her. I think you should let her make her own decision." Nicole shrugged out of her blanket and stood. Carefully, she made her way down to her snow machine, but before she drove away through the snowy woods that stood between this cabin and the one she shared with Link, she turned around on the seat and said, "You're no Miller McCall. You're better."

EIGHT

Kate shoved the covers off her legs, utterly frustrated with her inability to sleep. She'd even counted sheep in desperation, but as she'd almost drifted off, she imagined a wolf chasing the sheep and got upset all over again. She'd spent an hour with her watercolors painting, but that hadn't even settled her enough.

She'd never in her life had trouble sleeping until Miller McCall, and she was desperate to get back to that. She wanted it all—good dreams, that well-rested feeling in the morning, not dragging all day, and looking less exhausted. It had been two years since she'd seen Miller. Two years the man was dead, and she was still as pathetic as she was when he was around. She'd spent too many nights waiting for him to break into her place and hurt her, she supposed. Too many nights feeling like the world was suffocating her and she was alone with her fear, and now her body was trained to never rest.

Dalton had changed that for a moment, and now she was downright desperate to have more of that warm, well-rested feeling.

She almost wished she'd never met Dalton. One day of relief had made her insomnia unacceptable now.

A soft knock sounded on the door, and she jumped. Fear dumped adrenaline into her system. Slowly, quietly, she opened the drawer to the bedside table and pulled out a machete she kept there. She slid the long blade from its nylon sheath and padded over the cold tile floors toward the door.

"Who is it?" she asked.

"It's Dalton."

Kate lifted one of the blinds on the door window with the tip of the curved blade. "It's late."

"I know."

"If this is some kind of booty call, I'm not interested."

Dalton locked his arms on the doorframe and frowned at the wall beside him. "I'm not here for that. I came to apologize."

"At four in the morning?"

"Were you asleep?"

Irritated, she sighed, flipped on the light, and opened the door. "No."

Dalton straightened up. "If I met you a month from now, things would be different. I would be different. Better. Easier. Not so…fucked up."

"Everyone is effed up, Dalton. At some point, you just have to find someone to share the baggage with."

He chuckled and scratched the side of his lip with his thumbnail, attention on the machete in her hands. "You would get along well with Nicole."

Jealousy snaked through her like a poisonous green fog. "Is she your ex?"

His nostrils flared softly, and a smile stretched his lips. "Possessive," he accused. "Two days with me and already—"

"Stop it. Don't joke right now. I was hurt tonight. Pushed aside. Pushed away. You kissed me and took me out and then kept me at a distance."

The smile faded from his face. "I know."

"Come inside so I can lay into you properly without letting all the heat out."

Dalton inhaled deeply and strode past her like he was headed for the chopping block. Dutifully, he sat on the couch, rested his elbows on his knees, clasped his hands, and waited.

Kate tossed the machete onto the table, and it clattered over the stack of sketches and paintings she'd been working on. "I like you. A lot."

Dalton's eyes narrowed suspiciously. "This isn't how I thought this would go."

"Shhh. I thought about you today to the point of distraction. I don't know why. You look half out the door already, ready to run away at any moment. I know you don't feel the same about me, but still, my stupid heart latched on."

"Is this the part where you tell me you hate me?" he asked, looking utterly baffled.

"What? No. I would never say that. I'm trying to explain how much I disliked you bolting for your truck when we dipped into a serious conversation. Who said they hated you?"

"Well…" He frowned. "My ex."

"Well, your ex sounds like a bit—" Kate stopped herself, swallowed the curse down, and sat in the chair across the coffee table from him. "She sounds like a bit of a handful."

Dalton canted his head like a curious animal. "Elyse is a friend, and Miller's death wasn't exactly handled by the police, if you catch my drift. You figured out where that scar on her face came from surprisingly easy, and it scared me." He dipped his voice lower. "*You* scare me."

She scared him? That was laughable. She was a buck-thirty of submissive human and he was a danged werewolf whose eyes had lightened to the color of caramel just now. She knew what kind of power he hid. Miller had been able to lift her off the ground by her throat like she weighed no more than air. "The feeling is mutual."

He watched her for so long she fidgeted and dropped her gaze. The air felt heavy around him now, making it hard to breath.

"Kate, I…" He swallowed hard, his Adam's apple dipping to the neck of his white sweater.

She waited for what seemed like hours as he struggled to say something. He scrubbed his hand down his dark stubble and sank back into the couch cushions. He was breathing too hard, looked panicked, so she stood, moved across the room, and sat next to him.

She searched his stunning eyes for a few seconds before she relaxed against his side and slid her arms around his waist. *Let me in.*

"I want to be a dad," he whispered, his body rigid as an ice sculpture beside her. "I always did. I lost—" Dalton inhaled sharply as though he couldn't breathe, so she loosened her embrace and rested her cheek on his chest. "I lost a baby. A girl. There's something wrong…with me. I can't make children right. The girls get sick. And I knew that going into the pregnancy with my ex. We got pregnant accidentally, but I was so fucking happy when she told me. She was scared, and I wasn't scared enough. I was convinced it was a boy. That I couldn't have a loss like that. Not me. I'd been a good person. I thought that was it, the family I always wanted. I wasn't ready at all, didn't even want an ultrasound to determine the sex because I was just that confident it was a boy. I was cocky. Or maybe deep down I was too scared to find out, I don't know." Dalton wrapped his arms around her, too tight, but she kept quiet. "The day she was born, I felt like someone had hit me in the middle with a hammer. We'd packed baby clothes to bring her home, but the second the doctor said it was a girl, my entire world burned. I knew we wouldn't be taking her home. And my ex wasn't bonding with her. She wasn't looking at her. Wasn't looking at me, like she knew I'd failed her and ruined our family. Or at least, that's what I thought at the time because I blamed myself completely, so it made sense that she did, too. I held her…" Dalton dragged in a long breath, so Kate held him closer. "I held her all night, listened to every breath because I knew what was coming. And I loved her so much. I wanted her to live. I prayed that I could die instead. I got one day with her. It was quick. Shelby didn't cry. She was in shock maybe, I don't know. She held her little body afterward because the doctors said it was good for her to do that for closure, but she didn't seem interested, and I couldn't hold her anymore. Just couldn't. I didn't want to feel her cold." Dalton let out a shaky breath. "Shelby broke it off with me then."

"April first?"

"Yeah."

"What was her name?"

Dalton rested his cheek against the top of her head and whispered, "Amelia."

"Beautiful name."

"For a beautiful girl. She was perfect. Dark hair, dark eyes. She looked Ute, like me."

"Ute? I thought you were Alaska Native."

"Nah, I'm Native American. I look like the first Ute in my lineage, Ukiah Dawson. I have pictures of him. My cousin got none of the Ute looks. He looks like a blond Viking and Shelby was blond, too, so I thought I would have a fair-haired baby. I like that Amelia got my traits."

"You marked her up good," Kate murmured.

97

He let off a soft chuckle. "Yeah."

Carefully, she straddled his lap, then tucked her arms underneath her and snuggled against his chest. Dalton hugged her close, and little by little, his heartbeat settled into a steady, thrumming rhythm under her.

"Thank you," she said.

"For what?"

"For telling me about Amelia."

"Yeah, well, someone once told me I have to find someone to share my baggage with."

"Whoever told you that sounds like a genius."

Dalton snorted, then stood lithely with her in his arms. "Time to sleep, insomniac." He walked past the coffee table, but froze, then settled her on her feet slowly. "What's this?"

Horror seized her as he bent over and picked up one of the half-buried watercolor papers she'd painted. She hadn't hidden that one well enough because she'd never thought she would see Dalton again.

"Nothing," she rushed, pushing a stack of blank paper over the dark ink rendering of a red, black, and violet phoenix.

"Oooh, you have a big crush on me," Dalton said, pulling it from under the pile of paper shields she'd created.

She yelped and plucked the damning painting from his fingertips, just to have him yank it back and hold it too high for her to reach.

"This is badass," he said, studying it.

"I was inspired by your tattoo and was looking for something to paint, and this was a fun idea. I like phoenixes."

"A phoenix that looks just like my tattoo?" he asked, one eyebrow arched down at her.

"I don't like people seeing these. I'm not an artist. It's just something that helps me sleep. Sometimes."

Dalton folded the painting and shoved it in his pocket. "I'm keeping this."

"No, you're not!" She scrabbled for his pocket, but he angled away from her with a teasing grin.

"Too slow, tiny human."

Kate jolted to a stop, and Dalton's face shut down completely. He backed away a few steps.

"You should be more careful."

"I don't know what you mean," Dalton said. A growl rattled his throat, but he shook his head hard, and the noise cut off.

He was giving her Amelia, but he was keeping the wolf.

Kate swallowed down bile at what she was considering. He wasn't telling her, and he had his reasons. Reasons she couldn't comprehend. But he was hinting. Baby girls dying? That must be a werewolf thing. Calling her tiny human? Growling? Allowing her to see his blazing eyes now? He was telling her without telling her.

"Don't run." Dang her voice as it trembled, but she was scared. If she let him know she knew, would he kill her? Would he be forced to silence her by whatever laws he and his people abided by? Would he leave and never come back? Miller, Miller, Miller. That man had been crazy and would've killed her if he knew she knew. Would Dalton react the same? No. She had to believe he wouldn't. Had to believe her heart wouldn't fail her twice. Slowly, she turned around and peeled her thin, red, cotton night gown over her head. She wore panties but no bra so her shameful scar would be visible.

Shaking, she covered her breasts to feel less vulnerable, even though he couldn't see them with her back to him.

She didn't hear him approach, but she knew he was there, standing just behind her. A soft touch traced the shameful bite mark in the middle of her back.

"Who besides Miller has seen this?" he gritted out.

"Just you."

"Did you ask for it?"

She couldn't breathe, couldn't move. Couldn't release a single word because admitting this would expose her feelings of helplessness.

Dalton turned her slowly, then hooked a finger under her chin and forced her gaze to his. "Did you?"

"No," she choked out. "I thought…"

"Say it."

She closed her eyes, because the fury in his face was terrifying.

"I thought I would turn into one of you. For months, I lived in fear that he would come back and hurt me again. That he would come back and kill me. That I would turn out to be just like him."

"Open your eyes." When she did, he said, "That's not how it works."

"Well, Miller didn't exactly explain anything. The sex was consensual, but the bite was not. He left afterward, laughing. He said I was stuck with him now, and I would make a pretty little breeder."

"That's not how this works either," he ground out.

"He disappeared. Or…died. And I didn't Turn. I figured I was safe when nothing happened."

"Who have you told?"

"Only you."

Dalton's eyes were so light, a blazing gold now. "Just so you know how I am, so you know what I'm capable of, if Miller was alive, I would avenge you. I would kill him, and then I'd leave his body for the ravens to pick clean. I wouldn't have any regrets taking his life. If that scares you, tell me to leave."

"You do scare me."

Dalton took a step back, acceptance slashing through his inhuman eyes.

"But not because of what you are. I'm scared because I don't want you to hurt me."

"I won't."

"You will if you run. If you leave. If you realized I'm not enough, like everyone else does."

"You aren't scared of the animal?" he asked.

"Should I be?"

Dalton shook his head slowly back and forth. "He's yours."

"Are *you* mine?" she whispered.

Chest heaving, Dalton dipped his chin once.

Relief was a tidal wave washing through her. Closing her eyes, she sighed at how amazing it felt to be wanted. "Good."

When she opened her eyes again, Dalton was pacing beside the couch, wild eyes on her.

"Come here," she murmured.

He was to her in three long strides. His hands gripped her waist as his lips crashed onto hers, urgent and possessive. She opened for him because she understood. She'd felt this way when he'd mentioned Shelby, and she'd just shown him the mark on her back. She didn't know what the bite meant, not yet, but it was big. It angered Dalton.

His tongue pressed into her mouth in smooth strokes as he ran his fingertips up her ribcage and cupped her breast. With a moan, she arched against him. Dalton eased back just far enough to work his sweater over his head, then pressed against her, skin to skin. He was so impossibly warm, felt so incredibly right touching her. Breasts aching for him, she gripped his hair and eased him downward. His lips were perfect, sucking, biting down her neck as he ran his hands down the sides of her arms, drawing gooseflesh where he connected with her. She gasped as his mouth clamped onto one of her sensitive nipples, drawn up tight in arousal. His tongue laved over and over until her knees buckled.

With a growl, Dalton straightened up, taking her with him as he walked her to the bed. His arms were flexed and sexy where he held the backs of her knees, and when he laid her on the mattress, he followed. He ripped her panties like they were paper, then threw them on the floor. She was writhing, begging with her body as he worked his kisses down her stomach. She drew her knees up and spread her legs for him as he bit her gently on the inside of her thigh.

"Eat me," she begged.

His chuckle reverberated against her skin. So close. "Brave little human, commanding the wolf to eat you."

He gave her a flash of those beautiful gold eyes before he slid his tongue up her wet slit. She bucked against him and gripped his hair. A soft growl reverberated from his lips as he pushed his tongue deep inside of her. He stroked into her until the pressure was too deep, too bright. His teeth brushed her sensitive clit, and he sucked once.

"I'm going to come," she said.

Dalton pulled away from her immediately and when he climbed over her, his pants were undone. Excitement filled her as he lowered his hips to hers.

"So close," she murmured, rolling her hips against his, silently begging for him to fill her.

Dalton clamped his teeth on her neck and snarled. When he released her skin there, he pushed the head of his cock into her, then eased out.

"Dalton!"

He gritted his teeth and pushed deeper. Tingling pressure was already building again. He felt so good inside of her, so big, stretching her, so long. How was he this long? His abs flexed against her belly as he slid fully into her.

"Oooh," she moaned, raking her nails down the rigid curves of his arms.

Dalton was losing control, bucking harder, faster. So sexy.

"Harder," she dared him on a breath, because if she was going to come this fast, she wanted him right there with her.

Dalton slid his arm around her backside and slammed into her again and again. He leaned down and kissed her, then gritted his teeth against her lips. "Uh," he grunted as his cock swelled inside of her. He went rigid and yelled out her name as the pressure became blinding. Orgasm exploded through her, pulsing around him as he shot hot streams inside her. She met him blow for blow as he emptied himself, driven to madness with the intensity of her pleasure and a little spark of pain in her chest.

"Dalton," she said in a whisper as she ran her fingernails down his back. He felt vital now. In this moment, he was everything.

Dalton bucked into her a few more times, then slowed down and kissed her softly. He rested his forehead on hers, eyes closed as he let off a long sigh. Rolling over, he took her with him and hugged her tight to his chest. "I shouldn't have taken you like that. I should've drawn it out for our first time."

She smiled against his chest, still shocked at what they'd just done. At how perfect it had felt. "I liked our first time just how it was. Dalton?"

"Hmm?"

"I want you to trust me."

He grew quiet for a long time, and his breathing evened out as she lay snuggled against him. But just when she thought he'd fallen asleep, he kissed the top of her head and let his lips linger there. "I'm a werewolf," he whispered.

Kate tightened her arms around him and smiled. "And what am I to you?"

Dalton's heart raced faster under her cheek. When he leaned back, she could see the waves of emotion there in his light gold eyes. Surprise. Regret. Acceptance. Tenderness. Adoration. Then lastly, honesty. He whispered, "You're my mate."

Nestling closer, she kissed him, a reward for not running. "Good."

"Yeah? And what am I to you?"

"The human equivalent. You're my man."

"Your man," he rumbled. "I like that."

Before she could chicken out, she blurted out, "What does my scar mean?"

Dalton softly traced the raised circular shape near her spine. "If it was consensual, which is how it is supposed to be done, you would've been his claim. No one else could touch you. No other shifter, or he would have rights to challenge them."

"Challenge them how?"

"To the death."

She propped up on one elbow and frowned. "I don't understand why he did it. He didn't really like me that much. He wasn't nice to me at the end. That's when he bit me, at the end."

"McCalls go crazy. It's bad genetics, a bad bloodline. Miller hunted a friend of mine."

"Elyse?"

"Yeah. Her mate was hibernating—"

"Hibernating?" she yelped.

Dalton chuckled. "Wolves aren't the only shifters."

"So Ian Silver is what? A bear?"

"Grizzly. He doesn't hibernate anymore. There is a cure for that now, but the first year he and Elyse were together, Miller called his entire insane pack to hunt her."

"Why?"

"Because the Silver brothers are the enforcers for shifters. If one of us does wrong to humans, like Miller and his brother Cole did, the Silver brothers are ordered to go in there and protect humans. After Ian fulfilled a kill order on Cole, Miller went after him and Elyse as revenge."

"Enforcers keep the peace by killing them?"

"By putting them down. McCalls usually get themselves put down sooner or later. Miller chased his own death by going after Ian. Elyse is a warrior, and one of the pack turned on Miller. He helped Elyse."

"Who?"

"Lincoln McCall."

"Your alpha."

Dalton smiled down at her. "You sure do understand a lot about a lot."

"You weren't very careful with your secrets around me."

His darkening eyes danced and he nipped her nose. "Maybe I wanted to get caught by you." Dalton pushed out of bed, leaving her skin cold. He pulled the covers over her hips, leaving only her breasts bare, then strutted into her kitchen like a proud rooster. He glanced over his shoulder with that teasing, naughty smile of his. "I like the way you look, just like this. Hair wild, skin flushed, satisfied."

"Tits out."

"Yes, if you can figure out a way to always be tits out around me, I'd sure appreciate it." Dalton opened the cupboards and pulled down a couple of plates and glasses, then found the pans and opened the fridge like he knew exactly where everything was. "Where did you get bacon?"

"Hardware Jack," she answered, fluffing up her pillow beneath her cheek so she could better ogle the muscular curve of his back and butt. "He works at the—"

"Let me guess. The hardware store."

"Good doggy."

Dalton snorted and pulled a carton of eggs and the bacon from the fridge.

"He cut his hand on a saw last week, and he hates spending time in the medical center and doesn't have much money for it anyway, so we traded."

"Stitches for bacon?"

"Exactly."

"God, you're sexy."

"Says the hot, growly, tattooed, naked guy cooking breakfast in my kitchen right now. This is better than a porno."

He huffed a surprised laugh as he turned on the stovetop. "Have you watched many pornos?"

"You mean besides the one I starred in?"

The smile dropped from his face, and Dalton went quiet as he cracked several eggs into the pan.

"I'm sorry," she murmured. "I shouldn't bring that up."

"The video is gone." When Dalton crossed his arms and leaned back on the counter, the inhuman color was back in his eyes. "It's gone, Kate. You won't be haunted by what Miller did anymore."

"I don't understand."

"I called in a favor."

In a rush, she wrapped the blanket around her shoulders, stumbled out of bed, and ran for her laptop. Her fingers flew as she typed in the first address. It was some doggy-style-lovers website, but when she typed in her name, nothing came up. And when she typed the exact title of the video, a blank screen popped up that read *this video is no longer available for viewing.* What the heck?

She searched another website, and another. She typed her name into the search engine but got no results other than a couple of pictures she'd uploaded to a social media account a few years ago.

"How?"

"I have a friend with powerful connections. I owe him a favor now."

Her face crumpled as she stared at the glowing computer screen that no longer damned her family's name—that no longer damned her. She clapped the laptop closed and hugged it to her chest as tears streamed down her face.

And Dalton was there, rubbing her back. He'd moved too fast, but that didn't scare her. Miller's unnatural speed had terrified her, but Dalton was good. Miller had let her down and so had the police when she'd tried to report the video, a huge breach in her privacy. Her parents had been embarrassed so badly they'd pulled away, and her sister had been open in her disappointment.

But Dalton...

Without her even asking, Dalton had come into her life and fixed this awful event that had happened to her.

"When did you do this?" Her throat tightened with every word.

"After I left here."

"After you said goodbye? After you said I wasn't yours to worry over?"

Dalton hugged her from behind and kissed her neck. "Yeah. Turns out you *are* mine to worry over. I planned on leaving. I was going to go back to Kodiak. Let you carry on with your life and forget me, but I hated the way Miller hurt you with that fucking video."

"So you fixed it."

"Yeah."

Wiping her eyes, she turned and smiled at him, hugging the computer. "Thank you."

Dalton gave her a lopsided grin and kissed her quick, then strode for the kitchen to stir the steaming eggs. "Anytime, human."

Slowly, she set the laptop down and padded across the cold tiles until she reached him. The phoenix snaking down his back meant more to her now that he'd shared Amelia's story. He wasn't out of the ashes yet, but she was going to help him get there if it was the last thing she did. He deserved happiness after all he'd been through.

She laid tiny kisses on his back and hugged his waist from behind as he made them eggs and bacon. "You're a good man, Dalton."

He huffed a humorless laugh. "If you knew what I was thinking, you wouldn't say that."

"What are you thinking?"

Dalton didn't answer. Instead, he busied himself with filling their plates with breakfast. "What time do you work today?"

"I don't."

"Good." He gave her a bright smile, but it didn't reach his eyes.

Suspicious, she followed him to bed where he was carrying the plates.

"Dalton, what are you thinking?"

He bared his teeth, the look there and gone in an instant. It wasn't a smile or a grimace. It was an animalistic show of displeasure. Dalton set the plates on the crumpled covers and sat down, then pulled her waist gently toward him until she stood between his legs. "You'll think I'm a monster."

"I won't."

"You're human. You won't understand the instinct."

"I will if you explain it to me."

His eyes were full of disgust when he lifted his attention to her. Slowly, eyes on her, he leaned forward, pushed the blanket away from her naked body and kissed her belly. "I'm distracting you so you don't take a birth control pill."

"Dalton," she whispered.

"You want to know what I'm thinking? My wolf hopes you're pregnant. *I* hope you're pregnant." Dalton released her and gave her an empty smile. "And now you'll be the one running."

"You want to be a daddy."

"No, it's not just that. I've haven't wanted to have a baby with anyone since Shelby. I'm not in some mindless procreation mode where anyone will do. I want a baby with you." He rested a palm on her flat stomach. "Want to see *you* growing my pup. Holding my pup. Nursing my pup." His voice had gone growly and strained. "I know it's too soon, but my wolf doesn't care."

"And what if we had a girl?"

"Link and Nicole have a baby girl." Dalton winced in pain. "There's a cure. Too late for my baby, but Link got his."

"Oh my gosh," she murmured, pulling him in close as her heart ripped apart. To miss the cure by so little, and now his alpha had a girl baby.

As heartbreaking as his loss had been though, Kate wasn't capable of giving him what he desired so soon. She wasn't ready, but maybe someday. "Dalton, I want breakfast in bed with you. I want you to hold me, make me feel safe in that incredible way you do, and then I want to sleep beside you. Then I want a second date and a third, and I want to keep growing this bond between us because you feel so important to me, like we could have a great love story. Take care of me, and I'll take care of you, and someday, maybe, we'll get to the life you deserve."

Dalton cupped her cheek and kissed her. There was promise in it. Forgiveness that she'd denied him, gratefulness that she hadn't run, and adoration above all.

I love him. Oh, she did, but it was scary feeling so attached this soon. But with every tender kiss she could almost hear his feelings, and they ran as deeply as hers. They were just as terrifying, and yet he was still here, falling with her.

She wouldn't admit it now because they'd both been burned by betrayal and needed time to build trust, but she could imagine him holding their baby, and growing a family together. She could imagine his gold eyes in their smiling child's face.

Dalton's wants and her wants were one in the same. Only she wasn't governed by animal instincts, so she would be strong for them both until they were ready.

NINE

Kate smiled at the other nurse at the medical clinic. Lacy had been a godsend over the last few years as Dr. Vega's mood had plummeted. She could always count on an understanding smile from Lacy and occasional drinks at the bar after particularly brutal shifts.

Lacy grinned brightly. "Guess who just walked in?"

"Mr. Danvers?" He was a bit of a hypochondriac and came in most days with some imaginary ailment. Yesterday, he'd been convinced he was filled with bot flies, which didn't even live in Alaska.

Lacy giggled and shook her head. Shoving her hands in the pockets of her purple scrubs, she twitched her blond ponytail off her shoulder and leaned against the hallway wall. "Someone tall, dark, and sexy as fuck just asked for you up front. I think Janice will have to be admitted for exploding ovaries after this. You should go save her."

Kate laughed at the mental picture of Janice sitting at the front, trying to check Dalton in while flirting shamelessly. She was on the north end of sixty, but she was proof that age was just a number.

"So this is the second time he's come in here in a week," Lacy said conversationally. "And you've been smiling to yourself a lot."

"He makes me happy."

"Good. I approve of any man who gets you living again."

Kate let off a shocked sound. "I have been living."

"You've been working and throwing yourself into caring for everyone but yourself. It's good to see you back to your old self." Lacy winked and pushed off the wall.

Kate stared after her as she disappeared into the only occupied room at the moment, her sneakers squeaking loudly across the tile floors. Huh. Over the last week, she'd felt the changes in herself. The opening up, the laughing, the feeling comfortable in her own skin again, but Lacy was right. She'd found a bit of her old self again.

With an absent smile, Kate made her way to the front entrance and stifled a laugh as she saw Janice leaned against the counter, outside of her station, hand on Dalton's bicep, petting his muscles like a cat. Dear goodness, she was incorrigible. Dalton looked up and gave Kate a good humored help-me look before he returned his attention to Janice's open affection and responded to something she'd said.

He held a bouquet of red tulips at his side as he leaned on one elbow against the sterile, white counter, one ankle crossed over the other and looking every bit the epitome of confident male. Sexy Dalton. That's what she called him in her head.

Dr. Vega strode by and grabbed her arm, leading her to the mouth of an empty room.

"Ow," she whispered, yanking her arm from his grip, but he only held on tighter. "Let me go."

"What is he doing here?" Dr. Vega's hair looked even thinner today, stringy almost, and his complexion was pallid. His brow trickled with a drop of sweat, and his eyes were bloodshot, his pupils dilated.

"He's my…" She gritted her teeth. Dr. Vega would have to get used to Dalton because sometimes he would be picking her up from shifts, like tonight. "He's mine."

"I'd get your hands off her if you want to keep them," Dalton said blandly.

He was standing on the other side of the hall, just a few feet away. He had appeared without a sound, and behind her thick glasses, Janice looked utterly baffled that Dalton wasn't still under her outstretched hand, accepting her petting.

Dalton's posture was relaxed and his voice calm, but the gold fire in his eyes scared her on behalf of Dr. Vega. The doctor let her go with a small shove. He gave a cruel laugh and dragged his glare from Dalton to Kate. "He's yours?" His voice turned to ice as he leaned toward her and whispered, "You have no idea what you're doing. No idea who he is."

"You're wrong. I know him. I don't know you." And she was beginning to think she never had.

Dr. Vega turned with an empty half-smile on his lips for Dalton. "Mind the woods at night, *Dawson*. Alaska isn't safe for monsters anymore." He turned and sauntered off, leaving Kate rubbing her arm where he'd grabbed her and wondering what the hell had just happened.

"He's mad," Dalton murmured.

"I'll say."

"Not angry-mad, Kate." Dalton gave her a significant look and lowered his voice. "He smells like McCall madness without the wolf."

Fear snaked up her spine, lifting the fine hairs on her body.

"Are you almost finished with your shift?" he asked, lifting her sleeve to look at where she'd been rubbing the soreness. A soft growl rattled his throat as he saw the red marks from Dr. Vega's grip.

"Yeah," she murmured. "Slow day, only one patient right now, and I've already transferred her to Lacy. Let's get out of here." With every second she stood here, the uneasy feeling grew deep within her gut.

"You should report him, Kate. He shouldn't treat you like that. Shouldn't hurt you."

"Dalton," she whispered, "you heard what he called you." *Monster.* "I'm not going to battle with Dr. Vega until I figure out what he knows. He could have all of Galena armed with pitchforks if he feels pushed into it. You're mine to protect, too."

Dalton gave one last long, hard look down the hallway Dr. Vega had disappeared, then nodded once. Scrubbing his hand down his face, he sighed, then took her hand and placed it gently in the crook of his elbow until they reached the front. While Kate grabbed her purse from behind the counter and shrugged into her jacket, Dalton smiled politely and said his farewell to Janice.

Outside, the sun shone brightly, warming her cheeks, and apparently warming everything else because the snow was already half melted, and the rich scent of defrosted earth hit her nose. Mud-season was coming. As much as she looked forward to warm weather, she dreaded how swampy everything would become as the abundance of snow melted into the Alaskan countryside.

Without a word, Dalton lifted her by the waist over a river of runoff water streaming downhill beside the curb. Deep trouble lingered in his eyes as he opened the door of his truck for her.

"Sooo, that was weird," she said when he was settled behind the wheel.

"That man isn't right. And I sure as fuck don't like him mishandling you like that. Has he ever done that before?"

"Never. He saw you, and I guess it set him off. Dalton, you and your pack need to be more careful. The McCalls raised suspicions in this town with their erratic behavior. Miller did, especially. I thought the rumors would go away since he's been gone so long, but I've heard things before. Whisperings about Link."

"Saying what?"

"That he isn't natural. That he isn't human. It's a small town with long, dark winters and nothing better to do than tell ghost stories. And the people here love their lore. This town is half Alaska Native, Dalton. You understand, right? You're Ute. Your people have stories, too."

Dalton heaved an irritated breath and muttered, "Shit."

"Language," she teased half-heartedly.

"Oh, right. Holy shit."

She rolled her eyes, and her face stretched with a grin. "I like those flowers. Did you buy them for Janice?"

"For you, of course," he said, handing them to her. Lowering his voice, he murmured, "That woman is a freak. Do you know what a Passion Pretzel is?"

Kate sniffed the flowers too hard and coughed. "It's a sex position, right?"

"Yeah. She told me all about it and then invited me over for dinner. She called today Aphrodisiac Tuesday."

Kate cracked up, doubling over her laughter. "I think Janice is one of my favorite people in the world."

"She's very educational."

"You want to try the Passion Pretzel, don't you?"

"Hell yeah, I do, but we can't just now. I have a question. Well, some news and a question. And now a few concerns," he said, voice darkening as he stared at the front of the medical clinic.

"Let me worry about Vega. It's date night, and I want you to touch my butt and buy me guacamole."

Dalton pulled out of the parking space and muttered, "Woman, you keep talking like that and you'll find yourself thoroughly fucked in the back of my truck before we even get home."

She liked the way he'd said *home*. Wiggling into a more comfortable position against the seat, she gave a private smile and waved to Hardware Jack, who was closing up his shop for the day. Dalton had spent every night at her apartment for a week, and she was not only well-rested, but also utterly satisfied in the diddle department. "What's your news? Is it good?"

Dalton's lips pursed into a thin line. "I have to go back to Kodiak. I have a repeat party, a few bachelors who come up here for fishing, and they've asked for me again. Chance, Jenner, and my boss have been covering for me with my April First shit, but I have to get back to work." He gave her a pleading look. "It feels important to get back."

"Away from me?"

"No, for you. I make good money, but it's dependent on me guiding trips. Usually I take all of April off, but the kind of fishing trip I'm being hired for is my bread and butter."

"Do you need money?" she asked, remembering that she'd never paid him for sleeping over. Though, now that she thought about it, it felt a little prostitute-ish to pay him for what they were doing at nights to get her tired.

As if he could read her tumbling thoughts, he said, "I don't want your money. Never did. I want to be able to provide for you, though."

"Well, I don't need your money either, ridiculous man. I need you, and I thought I had a couple more weeks before you went back to work. Oh, good grief, I sound so selfish right now. You've never asked me to take a day off work, and here I am, asking you to turn down a good tour. I'm sorry."

"Tiny, beautiful human, don't you ever apologize for wanting to spend time with me. I'd be worried if you were indifferent to me being around or leaving. I did that before with Shelby." Dalton slid his hand over the top of her leg and cast a glance from the road in front of them to her and back. "I like you being sore about me going. And as for me wanting to provide for you, I'm not talking about paying the bills on your apartment, and I'll never ask you to quit working. I know you love your job, and I like that you're independent. I just mean, if you want to breed huskies for the Iditarod someday, well…I plan on being a part of that, and if we're both saving up, we can get you there faster."

"Dalton," she whispered in shock. "I was scared you were going to leave for Kodiak and not come back."

He flashed her a dimple-bearing smile and shook his head. "You don't see it yet, but you will."

"See what?"

"That I'm completely yours. I hate thinking about being away from you, but I've already talked to Tobias and Ian Silver. They're both bush pilots, and they said they can fly me back and forth on my time off. And it'll give them consistent income, too, between their deliveries."

"I can get all three of my shifts grouped together. I know I can. Lacy and the other nurses have offered to help me do that before so I could take some time off for myself. I could come visit you at Silver Summit, too. This could work," she said hopefully, because the thought of being separated for long jaunts of time was excruciating.

"It will work. Jenner owns half of Silver Summit Outfitters, and he is a guide there, too. His mate, Lena, lives in a cabin on Ian's homestead, just forty-five minutes from here, and they see each other often. They make it work. And in dark winter, the weather gets too bad to do tours, so we close down the lodge and get a few months off. I'm still in this, Kate."

Her stomach fluttered with happiness as the layer of worry about them working in different parts of Alaska slid from her shoulders. She'd been afraid of talking about the future with Dalton, but instead of running like the other men in her life had, he'd solved the problems she'd imagined. He was a good leader and a capable man who seemed to know just what he wanted. She loved how direct he was. Loved that after he'd let her in, told her about the family he'd lost and confirmed he was a werewolf, he'd been completely open with her over the last week. Sure, he was still hurting because of April First. She'd met him on the anniversary of his daughter's passing, and he'd been reeling. She didn't blame him for panicking at the beginning. She understood how hard it was to open a heart that had been stripped bare, put it in someone else's hands, and give them the power to inflict pain again.

Each day, she saw more and more of the man he was outside of April, and somewhere along the way, she'd fallen hopelessly in love with him. And despite the oncoming physical distance that would hover between them, he was still here, telling her without an ounce of hesitation that she was still his, still worthy, still worth the effort of planning a life together.

She loved that he hadn't expected her to quit nursing, pack up, and move out to Kodiak to wait for him to come back from guide excursions. She liked that he empowered her to chase her dreams. He didn't build up walls to keep her safe and still like others had done. Instead, he offered his strength and stood back to back with her against the world.

"You said you had concerns," she said.

"Well yeah, Vega makes me nervous. I know you can handle yourself, but damn, my wolf is clawing at my skin to go back there and fix the problem so I won't worry about you being safe when I'm out in the bush."

"I feel like the human half of you will come up with a better solution than ripping Dr. Vega's throat out on my behalf," she said dryly.

"I already have."

Of course, he had. Dalton wasn't wishy-washy with his decisions like she was, and he saw solutions where she didn't see any. Dr. Vega would live, but only because the human side of Dalton was strong in his logic. Miller had been missing that. He hadn't the impulse control Dalton had. Or the sanity.

Dr. Vega worried her, but perhaps he would back off whatever judgements he held when her mate was out of town and far out of his reach. Dalton would be safe, so as hard as it would be to spend a single night away from him, the distance would be worth it.

Dalton turned up the volume on Galena's radio station. A boy-band song filled the cab, and he nodded his head to the hard-hitting beat. "Aw, here we go. You ready?" He belted out a long, loud, off-key note to the song, instantly B-slapping any thoughts of Dr. Vega right out of her head.

Dalton was actually an incredible singer with a strong, steady baritone voice that made her swoon when he was humming to himself in her kitchen or in the shower, but this was their game. The How Bad Can We Sing game. She let off a giggle and swayed her arms while wiggling her hips, waiting for her part. And when the chorus came, she adopted a pirate voice and sang in an off-tune harmony with Dalton.

By the end of the song, they were gasping for air between laughs and horrible singing, and she had to wipe tears from the corners of her eyes.

Gosh, she adored him.

She grinned at him as he took a solo. She'd never in her life felt so comfortable around someone.

On the other side of him, through the open window, blobs of snow were falling from evergreen branches, and the woods outside of town had grown thick and wild. Dalton turned left on a muddy road out in the middle of nowhere.

"Where are you taking me?" she asked.

"To a cabin in the woods so we can play Erotic Red Riding Hood and the Big Badass Wolf."

"Dalton, in that story, the wolf plots to eat Red Riding Hood."

He turned a wicked grin on her and slid his hand farther up her thigh. "My wolf plots the same."

She parted her lips to call him a "ridiculous man," but he slipped his hand into the elastic waist of her scrubs and then under her panties until he cupped her sex. His middle finger brushed her clit, and she rolled her hips and relaxed against the seat. Pressing her palm over his hand to show him the pace she wanted, she let off a soft sigh and closed her eyes. She loved this, loved his touch. She would never tire of how he made her feel.

Dalton's breath became more uneven with every stroke of his finger, and when he had her soaking wet, he slammed on the brakes and threw the truck into park. With a feral snarl, he leaned over and kissed her, hard. As soon as he pushed his tongue past her lips, he slid two fingers inside of her. She pulled his hand harder against her sex, hips moving to meet him stroke for stroke. Orgasm exploded through her, pulsing quick and deep. When he'd drawn every aftershock from her sensitive body, she pulled his hand out of her panties and pushed his chest back against his seat. After shoving the console up and out of the way, she forced his tight, thermal sweater over his head to feel his skin.

She unsnapped the button of his jeans as he sat there with his palms up, like he still didn't understand how he wasn't finger-banging her anymore. The rip of the zipper was loud in the cab of his truck, and she shoved his pants down, unsheathing his long, thick erection.

"What are you—uuuuh," he groaned as she slid her mouth over the head of his cock.

He melted against the seat and rocked gently, his fingers entwining in her hair as she bobbed up and down, careful to keep her teeth from his skin while keeping pressure on him with her tongue and lips.

When she angled her head, his hips jerked. Too deep, so she gripped his base and slowed the pace. Dalton growled again and slammed his head back against the headrest. His powerful legs tensed every time she slid her mouth down his shaft, and now his hand was getting tighter in her hair. She loved this—loved him trying to maintain control but losing it inch by inch. She was causing that sexy, wild sound in his throat. It was because of her that he was thrusting into her mouth now, unable to help himself. The reason he gripped the steering wheel so tightly she could hear the creak of it over her head was because he was getting off on what she was doing. Big, masculine, powerful beast of a man, but he was turned on by her taking control, by her touch.

His erection was hard between her lips, his head swollen. The tip tasted salty, and he pushed her mouth onto him faster. "Fuck yes, harder," he gritted out, abs flexing against her cheek with every heaving breath he took. "Kate, I'm going to...fuck." His hips rolled smoothly faster and faster. "Kate, I can't stop. I'm gonna come. Get off now unless you want—uuuh!"

The first shot of salty heat drenched her throat. Dalton went rigid when she swallowed another stream and another. His body twitched as he released her hair and gripped the steering wheel with both hands. The leather of the wheel groaned under his grasp as he doubled over her and pushed his hips at her again with a groan. His body was stone for the span of a few heartbeats before he relaxed back against the seat again and heaved an exhalation. "God, you smell good."

She pulled off him and kissed his tip, then grinned up at him. "Like honey?" He always said that. She'd made sure to eat extra honey on her oatmeal in the mornings just because he was so sweet with his compliments.

"Like honey and pheromones. I love the way your body reacts to me."

"Hey, remember that one time Erotic Red Riding Hood ate the Big Badass Wolf instead?"

Dalton grinned and brushed a wayward strand of hair from her face. He searched her upturned face with content pooling in his lightened eyes. "You make me happy," he murmured.

"A blow job would make any man happy," she pointed out.

He chuckled and shook his head. "No, it's not just that. Being with you is different. It's bigger. It pulls at pieces of me I thought were dead."

Oh, she knew what he was really saying. Late one night, he'd told her about how Shelby had treated him. About how she'd withered under his touch and squirmed away until he finally gave up on affection. Shelby had managed to make someone who was warm and giving curl into himself and feel too repulsive to touch. A part of her hated Shelby. A part of her was grateful Shelby had been awful enough that Dalton was able to break whatever bond he'd forged with her.

A stream of sunlight filtered through the window, illuminating Dalton's perfect, stony abs and casting the crease between his taut pecs in shadow. When he smiled down at her, his canines looked fractionally longer, and sharper. He looked monstrously beautiful with gold flames for eyes and a wolfish smile. "You know what I'm about to tell you, don't you?"

Kate sat up and snuggled against his side, her heart pounding against her ribcage. "I hope I do."

"Will it make you run?"

"I'm not going anywhere."

Dalton tucked her hair back and leaned slowly into her. "I love you," he whispered, cheek rasping against hers, lips to her ear.

Rolling her eyes closed, she melted against him and reveled in the relief that followed those words.

He loved her. *Her.* She hadn't just imagined what was building between them. He really felt the way she did, and for the first time in her life, she felt like she was on the same page with someone else.

She kissed him softly, then eased back to bask in the inhuman glow of his eyes. "I love you, too."

TEN

Dalton cut the engine and pulled on his sweater. Kate glanced around the muddy woods with their patchwork of snow mounds clinging onto life. The sunlight filtered through the spruce branches and birch limbs, patterning the forest floor with yellow speckles.

"Where are we?"

"I want to show you something," Dalton murmured, his lips curved into a lingering smile from the important trio of words they'd just shared with each other.

He pushed open his truck door and jogged around the front, then helped her out onto the muddy road.

"I didn't wear the right shoes," she said, frowning down at her work tennis shoes.

"I've got you." Dalton bent slightly and folded her into his arms with little effort. After kicking the door closed, he strode with her up one of the well-worn muddy divots in the road.

"Why aren't we driving? The road looks passable."

"Because I don't want you to see this place for the first time through my truck window. I want you smelling the air. I want you feeling the breeze, and I have a question I want to ask while we stand on this land, not in my truck. This place should be felt, not just seen."

Utterly confused, she nodded and wrapped her arms around his neck. "Okay."

With long, smooth strides, Dalton crested a hill and halted, then set her down gently. Kate dragged her gaze from his striking face, stoic now with an edge of worry, to a clearing. In the center was a rustic cabin. It was small, but beautifully crafted with log walls, natural wood details, a sizeable front porch, and a large window on the side. A stone chimney crept up the front, right beside the porch, and smoke puffed steadily from the flue. Snowcapped mountains set a scenic background to the home, and behind was a smaller cabin, not much bigger than a large storage shed.

Kate inhaled the crisp, clean air, and let it off in a long, reverent sigh. "Oh, Dalton. Is this your den?"

"No," he murmured, turning her shoulders slowly until she was squared up to him. "But it could be ours."

"What?" she asked, glancing at the beautiful homestead and back.

"My alpha bought this place before he met his mate. She owns the deed to the next property over, and Link moved in with her when they got married, but he didn't let this place go. I called him last night and asked if he would accept offers, and do you know what he said?"

"Tell me."

Dalton swallowed hard, his eyes filling with some emotion she didn't understand. "He said he's been waiting for me and Chance to come home. He's been saving this place for one of us to make an offer."

"Oh my gosh," she whispered.

Dalton slid his grasp from her arms to her hands and squeezed. "I live in a temporary room up at Silver Summit, and I've never looked into settling outside of the time I work. Not until I met you. I want to build a life with you, Kate. I'm selfish. I know you would have made a safer life if I'd been strong enough to leave you alone, but I can't do anything about that now. You feel like mine. My mate, my future, the one I want to come home to between jobs."

She opened up her mouth to share his sentiment, but Dalton got a panicked look and rushed on.

"I know it's fast. You're human, and you need time to feel the certainty I do. My wolf has bonded to you…I have bonded to you, and for the rest of my life, I won't see anyone else but you. But you don't have the animal, and you'll need time to build up confidence in me, and that's okay. I'll wait as long as you need me to. I can buy this place with my own money, put it under my own name if that will make it easier for you. You'll have an out. It's two cabins on sixty acres where my wolf can run safely, and you'll have the protection of my pack and my alpha when I'm away. Link and Nicole live down that trail." He jerked his chin at a worn path through the woods. "You don't have to wait on your dreams. We can purchase your first dogs, clear land for their shelters. You can start your sled training program if that's what you want to do. It's close enough to town that you could still keep up your shifts at the medical center. I have money in savings that can get us started. I have to keep working to keep up the payments, but I can give you this now."

"I have five thousand dollars saved up," she whispered through a tightening throat. Her eyes stung with tears at what he was offering her. "It wasn't enough on my own."

Dalton's eyes went wide, and he squeezed her hands harder. "What are you saying?"

She looked over the beautiful land and at the cozy cabin that was the home of her dreams. A deep connection was already forming inside of her as hope bloomed in her chest like a spring flower. "This place could really be ours?"

Dalton blew a shaky breath and nodded.

"Can I see inside?"

Dalton leaned down and kissed her, hand slipping behind her neck, thumb brushing her cheek. He sipped at her, then gave her tiny, loving pecks that ended with soft smacking sounds. They were the first sounds she heard here in this yard that could be the key to everything she'd always wanted, and now she understood his need for her to see Link's place like this—free of the truck engine noise pollution and distancing window glass.

He was asking and hoping for her to bond with this place and giving her the best opportunity to do so. With an emotional grin, she nipped his bottom lip.

"Why are your eyes watering?" Dalton asked, easing back by inches, eyes stricken with confusion.

"Because I'm happy."

"That makes no sense."

"Clearly you've been around the all boys' club way too long."

Dalton grinned and lifted her onto his back, holding her knees at his waist as he tramped across the muddy yard toward the cabin. "I'll give you that. Silver Summit doesn't have many female visitors. Happy tears don't exist there. Only happy beers."

She climbed down his back and onto the sturdy porch, kicked out of her shoes, then took a steadying breath before she pushed open the door. At the entrance, she hesitated in awe.

The outside was picturesque, like some Alaskan post card people in Galena sent to family members in the lower forty-eight. But inside this home, great care had been taken in the craftsmanship. The walls were logs, sanded to smooth surfaces and stained a beautiful chocolate brown color that contrasted with the gray sealant between each one to keep the weather at bay. The stones on the fireplace matched the ones outside, and the couch was made of dark leather. Every detail in this place gave it rich character. From the hand-carved coat rack, to the wooden counters, to the open concept. There were no walls separating rooms, only supportive beams that matched the exposed rafters above. Even the bedroom was only separated from the living area by a step up, and above the queen-size bed was the gorgeous picture window she'd seen from outside. From it, she could see the pine forest and the mountains jutting from the earth in the background. A fire crackled in the wood burning stove, the bed was made with a thick, red and beige plaid comforter, and white, simple dishes sat in a drying rack on the kitchen counter near the stainless steel sink. On a rustic carved table, outdoor magazines were scattered across the scratched surface, giving the place that lived-in feeling. It looked like a picture in a book. Staged, but homey. Perfect.

She could feel Dalton watching her, gauging her reaction, but she'd gone blank with the realization that this place could be where she slept. Where she lived and cooked and got ready for work in the mornings. This could be the place she greeted Dalton when he came home from guided tours.

Home.

This could be home.

"Wow," she whispered, taken aback with how much she already loved this place. "Do you want to hear something strange?" she asked as she stepped carefully onto the solid wood floor inside.

Dalton slid his arms around her waist from behind and murmured against her ear, "I want to hear everything."

"I've looked for cabins before. I even had a realtor, but none of the properties felt right. None of them fit." She rested her cheek against his, the softness of her face contrasting with the scratch of his short stubble. "This one does."

"Maybe you weren't meant to connect with those other cabins."

And suddenly, everything made so much sense. She'd never given a single thought to fate before. She'd been so bogged down with regret and bad decisions in men and friends, she'd never given a spare thought about bigger pictures. Everything she had done, experienced, and every ounce of pain had led her to this moment. Her ex, Nadine's betrayal, her desperation to feel wanted, and her unfortunate choice in Miller. Her distrust in people and need to take care of others in secret. These things had twisted her like a wire and made her a better match for Dalton. He deserved a strong mate. Required one to withstand the complications of his life and his animal, and she'd grown stronger over the past several years for this, right here. So she could see the reward. So she could appreciate the man she was meant for.

"I want to show you something," he murmured, taking her by the hand and leading her toward an open trapdoor off the kitchen.

"A root cellar inside?" she asked, excited by the treasure of not having to walk out in the freezing winter to gather the foods she wanted to cook.

"There's more." He climbed down the tall ladder, then helped her off the bottom rung when she climbed down after him. The floor was composed of packed earth, but the walls were made of old stone that looked to have been repaired many times over the years. Surprising because she hadn't realized the cabin was that old.

"Link rebuilt and repaired this place, but it was originally a moonshiner's cabin."

"They made moonshine in the root cellar?" she asked, confused.

Dalton pushed a small lever on the wall, and with a deep, echoing click, an entire wall of shelves, canned food and all, lurched forward. He gestured for her to open it the rest of the way. Enthralled, she pulled the panel to expose the entrance to a tunnel, propped up by railroad ties like some mining cave.

"Link calls it the fox tunnel."

"For the moonshiners to escape out to their caches in the woods without being followed and robbed or worse," she guessed.

"Exactly. It was part of why Link bought this place. He's mostly animal, or was before Nicole and the McCall Reset. He settled here more easily because it had an extra escape route. The end of the tunnel empties into the woods two hundred yards off. He told me about it when I asked about making him an offer on the house. Will you meet my pack?" he asked suddenly.

Surprised, she dragged her eyes away from the dark tunnel and up to his face. "When?"

"Now. They're waiting to meet you."

"I thought you said it wasn't a real pack. You said you were only bound by technicality."

"It started that way, but it's not the way Link wants it. He is part of the reason I began to consider this cabin. He wants us around more. Chance and I help keep him steady. We help him fight the McCall madness, along with a cure Vera made for his damaged DNA. I used to resent risking my own wolf's sanity to protect his, and then I resented him for keeping his own baby girl when mine had missed the cure. It's selfish. I was hurt and couldn't see anything but the shit I'd gone through. But I feel different now."

"Different about what?"

"Everything."

"What's changed?"

Dalton straightened his spine and shrugged. "I don't know. You. The pack. What I want from life. I went a long time making sure I stayed safe. Never connecting with people so I couldn't get hurt. And then I was thrown into this pack in exchange for the cure for werewolf females, and I fought hard to stay separate. I fought off any bond Link tried to make with me. I didn't hold his child, didn't let myself get close to his mate. They tried to build a good pack, and I sabotaged it."

"Dalton, you didn't sabotage it. You went through trauma, and you wanted to make sure it didn't happen again. It's a scary thing, giving people power over you."

"You did it. You let me in immediately, even after how Miller treated you."

"You're worth the risk."

He smiled and searched her face. "It's you, Kate. You caused the changes in how I feel. Keeping my distance from the pack won't just affect me. You'll be part of the pack, too. I'll hurt you if I keep us separate. I have to do better than I have been doing, for the pack, but also for you."

Pride unfurled in her chest, and she inhaled deeply, standing straighter with her growing admiration for him. April First didn't have Dalton on his knees crawling through the muck anymore. This was his stand to be better, to shoulder his pain, to take his life back, and to create something worth fighting for.

Dalton softening toward his pack told her more than any words he could say that he was in this with her. He wanted to fix what was broken, for her.

"I'd like that then. I want to meet your pack."

ELEVEN

"I should've brought a present. Wine or something. Hardware Jack makes watermelon moonshine. Maybe I should go back to town and get something."

Dalton grinned and shut the truck door behind her. He pulled her in close and clamped his teeth onto her neck, then released her with a sexy growl. "They won't need gifts to like you."

She giggled as her cheeks flushed with pleasure. "You're bringing a meek personality into a house full of werewolves and asking me not to be nervous."

"I'll be there," he murmured, backing away just far enough to let her see how serious he was. "I'll never let anything happen to you. And besides," he said, tugging her hand toward the small cabin that was glowing with lantern light from every window, "they don't bite. Much."

"You bite all the time."

"Love bites. And you should be counting your lucky stars with those. In the old days, a bite from a werewolf poisoned the blood and killed humans."

"What?" She skidded to a stop, just before the front porch. "Your bite could kill me?"

"No." He gave her a wolfish grin. "We evolved."

"Or *we* evolved. Maybe humans came up with an immunity to you."

Dalton frowned thoughtfully. "Huh. You should put that theory in front of Vera."

"The fox-shifter mad scientist?"

"Yeah, she eats that shit up. Of course, then she'll have you donating blood to her experiments to try and discover whatever antibodies you've built up over time if it's true. Maybe don't tell her if you want to avoid her needles. She's a freak for blood."

"She sounds terrifying."

"Nah, you'll get used to everyone."

Kate wrung her hands over and over and stared in fear at the front door. "I have a submissive personality. Am I the only one like me in your pack? And with the Silvers?"

"Woman, being submissive isn't a bad or good thing. It's just a personality type. Packs can't function if every single member is a dominant. We'd be bleeding each other all the time. It would be really hard for Chance, Link, and I to get along if Nicole wasn't around. You'll soothe us even more. Or…" He arched an eyebrow and smirked. "Maybe you'll jack up our protective instincts, and we'll be thrown into chaos."

"Is that supposed to make me feel better?"

He led her onto the porch and rapped his knuckles on the door, too hard. "I'm going to Passion Pretzel you tonight."

"Dalton!" she yelped as the door swung open.

A tall, Nordic-looking man with blond hair and bright green eyes stood there with a cocky half-smile. "Passion Pretzel, huh?"

Mortified, she ducked her gaze to the toe of her sneakers as her cheeks lit on fire. Dalton pulled her forward, and she almost stumbled into the man. "I-I like pretzels. Salted with ch-cheese dip."

Dalton let off a single, booming laugh as though what she said was the funniest thing in the world. She stomped his foot and wished with all her might she could grow the teats to glare at him right now.

Dalton didn't even flinch away from her stomp. "This is my cousin, Chance. Sarcastic asshole, terrible beer pong player, least important member of the pack."

Dalton lurched backward beside her, and she ghosted a glance just in time to see him recovering from a hard shove by Chance.

The giant Viking man leaned down and lifted her knuckles to his lips. "Chance Dawson, sex god, dominant badass, and professional at the Passion Pretzel."

A snarl ripped from Dalton beside her. "Don't you lay your fucking lips on her, man."

Chance grinned up at Dalton as the air grew heavy around them, then quick as a whip, he pecked her hand.

"Aaah!" she cried as Dalton and Chance blurred past her and ended up in the yard.

A tall woman with long, glossy black hair and a dark red birthmark that covered half her face appeared in the doorway. She let off a very non-intimidating, human growl and looked tired. "Not again."

"They're fighting," Kate said on a shocked breath. She winced as Dalton smashed his fist against Chance's jaw.

A humorless laugh echoed through the clearing and Chance grinned, teeth red, just before he spat crimson onto a melting pile of snow. And then he tackled Dalton.

"Come on inside. They might be at this for a while."

"Because of me?"

"Because they're bloodthirsty hellions who are in a constant fight for dominance. They'll be fine. I'm Nicole."

"Kate," she murmured.

She allowed Nicole to lead her inside and help her out of her jacket, but didn't remove her attention from the brutal fight until the door was closed. And when she turned around, a tall man with dark hair and light gray eyes looked down at her. There was no smile on his face, no spark of humor in his eyes like with Chance. His appealing face was marred with a fierceness that scared her.

"You were my brother's," Lincoln McCall said in a too gravelly voice.

Kate dropped her gaze and clasped her hands in front of her. The heavy air was worse in here, making it hard to breathe. "Miller and I dated yes, but I wasn't ever really his. Not like I am with Dalton. I was only Miller's plaything."

"I couldn't help you then."

Shocked at his words, Kate dared a look at him. The hardness in his eyes and the set of his jaw had lessened.

"What?"

Link stood straighter with his hands behind his back. "I watched what Miller was doing to you and the others, but I wasn't alpha. He was."

"You wanted to help me?"

Link dipped his chin once as Nicole wrapped her hand around the inside of his bicep and leaned against him.

"You weren't responsible for his actions, you know," Kate whispered. "He was."

"He said he bit you."

Kate closed her eyes tightly against the shame. "He did, but someday, Dalton's bite will cover it up, and then you and I will be absolved of our guilt."

"You aren't angry?"

She shook her head and forced herself to meet his eyes. "Not anymore. Miller made me ready for Dalton."

She didn't have to explain beyond that because Link's shoulders relaxed and a slow smile curved his lips. He held out his hand for a shake. "Link, alpha of the Galena pack."

Swallowing down her fear of touching someone who felt so heavy, so scary, she gripped his hand and shook it gently. "Kate Hawke, mate to Dalton Dawson, and someday," she said on a breath, "a hopeful member of your Galena pack."

A baby cooed in the other room, just a tiny sound, but the effect it had on Link was instant. His attention jerked to a bedroom door, his wolf just under the surface, alert, frozen, all instincts focused on that soft sound.

Nicole excused herself and rushed into the other room, then returned with a baby against her chest. "Shh-shh-shh,"

Nicole said, bouncing and shifting her weight from side-to-side.

The little girl was wearing a purple, cotton, one-piece pajama set and was kicking her legs robustly. When Link took her from Nicole's arms, Kate was helpless to take her gaze from the alpha and his daughter. He had melted like ice in spring, and his lips stretched into an adoring smile as the baby quieted in his arms. She had gray eyes only a couple shades darker than her father's and a dark crop of hair on her head. And on her jaw and neck, she had a birthmark the same dark red color of her mother's.

"She's beautiful," Kate whispered as she was drawn step-by-step toward the infant.

"She's my little warrior," Link murmured in a doting voice. "This is Fina."

Unable to help herself, Kate pressed her index finger against Fina's palm, and the tiny baby closed her fist around her touch.

"You want to hold her?" Link asked.

"Really?"

A long, low growl rattled from Link, and the air grew even harder to breathe. "She'll be fine," he said to no one in particular.

Nicole plucked the baby from Link's arms and settled her into Kate's. "He is talking to Wolf. His animal is protective, but he'll settle down when he sees you're okay with his pup."

Voice trembling, she said, "Okay. I promise I won't drop her." Kate swayed from side to side and smiled down at the round-eyed baby, who seemed riveted by the pair of pearl drop earrings she was wearing.

Carefully, she sat on the couch as Nicole took the seat beside her. Across the room, Link opened the door and let off a shrill whistle.

"Don't you get blood on my floors," Nicole called as the open doorway shadowed with the massive forms of the Dawson wolves.

Chance filed in first, lip split and face gory, but he was wearing a grin like he hadn't just been fighting in the yard. Dalton came in after, his cheek cut and freely bleeding, but other than that, looked unscathed. He was wearing a matching grin and chuckling. Suddenly, Kate realized she might never understand men. Or "bloodthirsty hellions," as Nicole had called them.

"Dalton, that looks bad," Kate said. "You need stitches."

He arched his attention to her, and the smile faded instantly from his face. His too-bright eyes dipped to Fina in her arms. "Won't need stitches. I heal fast. I'm going to wash up."

They all watched as he disappeared into the washroom, but it was Nicole who broke the thick silence. She patted Kate's leg comfortingly and cast her a sympathetic look. "Being around Fina is a reminder. It's hard on him. He's not mad at you."

Kate snuggled Fina closer, then settled her back in Nicole's arms. "Excuse me," she said as she made her way to the bathroom. Inside, she shut the door after her.

Dalton was standing near the sink, his back to her, arms locked against the counter, eyes cast down as though he didn't want to look at his reflection in the mirror. He inhaled deeply, then turned and gave her a pitiful attempt at a smile.

"I'm sorry," she said, approaching slowly. She slid her arms around his back and rested her cheek against his chest. Dalton's heart was pounding too fast.

Running his fingertips through her hair, he said, "Nothing to be sorry about. It was a beautiful thing, seeing you holding a baby."

"Not just a baby, Dalton. Fina."

His jaw clenched for a moment before he repeated, "Fina."

She took the dark washcloth that was dripping in his hand and gently washed the blood from his face, but Dalton had been right. He didn't need stitches. The wound was already closed and looked like a two-week-old scar. "I can't believe you fought Chance immediately after I met him," she admonished, dabbing his cheek dry.

"If I didn't, he'd be sneaking kisses on you just to piss me off. Now he won't."

"Monster," she teased.

Dipping down, he kissed her hard and when he pulled away, his eyes sparked with something hard. "You have no idea."

TWELVE

Dalton was losing his control.

He didn't know if it was from the fight with Chance, the fact that he hadn't Changed in a few days, or if it was being in this house with Link. Maybe it was from upsetting his mate. She'd been quiet during dinner, though not with the others. With them, she'd laughed and even told a couple of stories about life growing up breeding sled dogs. She'd charmed the pack, he could tell. Even now, her cheeks were nearly as red as her hair, but she was still daring glances at the others, who couldn't seem to take their eyes off her. Likely, she was an anomaly to them, as she had been to Dalton at first. Submissive she might be, but iron strength made her bold in surprising ways. She was witty and smiled easily. She looked so utterly human, sitting beside him in her purple scrubs, smiling shyly at all the banter between them, but she held the attention of the pack like she was a bug light and they were a tiny herd of mosquitos.

Something about her attracted people. Maybe it was her inner glow or the instinct that told creatures like him she housed a good soul, but watching his pack laugh, cater, and build rapport with her, he knew that she harbored something otherworldly that attracted darker beings like him, just to see if her goodness would rub off on them. Miller had sensed that in her, too, but had exploited it. He'd tainted her, jaded her, and tried to turn her dark like himself. Thank God Kate's light was stronger than the dark.

Dalton pulled her empty plate onto his own as a silent apology for how he'd acted earlier. He would have to Change tonight, and he'd never explained to Kate about the mood swings that came right before the wolf took his body. The hurt on her face had gutted him.

Fina called out in a sweet voice from the other room. Nicole had put her down for bed before dinner, but all the noise was apparently keeping her awake. Pretty baby. Sweet. She wasn't even crying, just calling out for attention. His grip tightened on the napkin in his lap as a memory of Amelia's face flashed through his mind like a lightning strike. Gulping down a snarl, he glanced at the cracked door of the dark bedroom for the hundredth time since they'd sat down for dinner.

His chest hurt. Burned, really, like each soft noise from the child added gasoline to the embers in his heart.

Fina settled, and Dalton blinked rapidly in relief, then smiled absently at some story Chance was telling about how they'd gotten drunk on his father's whiskey one summer and got lost in the woods for an entire night. It was a funny story, sure, but he wasn't in the mood for laughing.

Kate smelled good. Like honey and sex after what they'd done in his truck earlier. He couldn't wait to see her swell with his child someday. *Stop it.* Dalton shook his head to quiet the long growl in his throat.

Fina was calling out again, and for the hundred and first time, Dalton stared at that damned door again.

Kate pressed a soft kiss against his neck. Brave mate, showing affection like this in front of everyone. She inhaled deeply, snuggling him. She smelled worried. He was messing this up. Ripping his gaze away from Fina's door, he pressed a kiss onto Kate's hair and murmured, "I love you," because she should hear that after he'd been coarse with her earlier.

Across the table, Nicole looked sad now. She'd gone quiet, watching him, waiting for something he didn't understand. Link settled his elbows on the table and stared at him, his eyes lightened to the color of snow. Crazy McCall, or at least he had been before Vera and Nicole had saved him.

Even Chance's story tapered off, and his cousin's green eyes went somber as he leaned back in the chair across the table.

Fina cried out again. He had the woodgrain on the door memorized by now. "Does she always fuss like this before she tires herself out?"

"Sometimes," Nicole said.

"You should hold her," Dalton ground out.

"She's not calling me." Nicole canted her head, her soft brown gaze steady on him. "She's calling you."

Dalton gritted his teeth and stood. Kate was still holding his hand, holding him steady so he didn't run from what they wanted him to do. It was April. He wasn't ready. Wasn't steady. Wasn't capable.

Coward.

Stupid wolf. He didn't see how this would rip him up. Couldn't see how filling his arms with a child would bring everything back.

Everyone was staring, watching him stand frozen, connected only to Kate. He would go just to escape their stares, and then they would leave him the fuck alone. It was a good plan.

His hand slid from Kate's, and he strode into the dim room, lit only by a single nightlight in the corner. Pressing his back against the wall just inside the doorway, Dalton let off a long sigh, but it didn't help. His chest was filling with lead.

Fina's soft voice cooed over and over, as if she could sense him there. Tiny siren.

Helplessly, Dalton padded to her crib and looked over the edge. She'd kicked out of her blanket. Tilting her little chin back, she let off a long note, like a little wolf howl. Nicole had been right. She'd been calling him because now his inner wolf was silent, watching, not snarling and scratching at the surface of his skin.

Maybe she was cold. Dalton reached in and brushed his finger tip over the top of her foot, but it was warm. And so soft. Fina smiled. No teeth, gummy, so cute. So perfect. When pain slashed through his chest, he inhaled sharply. Carefully, he stroked the birthmark on her jaw. She was the first female werewolf, not Amelia, and there was nothing that could be done about that. It wasn't his fault. It wasn't Fina's.

She swung her chubby little fists around, and he caught one. She gripped his finger tightly, as if she wanted him here.

Eyes blurring, he reached in with both hands and picked her up. She let off another happy coo when he cradled her to his chest. Soothing tendrils spread through his body from where she rested against him.

Dalton backed up a few steps and sat on the edge of the bed. Fina kicked and talked, her eyes wide and clear and trained on him like he wasn't a monster. He doubled over her and squeezed his eyes closed. Tears streamed down his face, but he didn't care.

"You have me," he rasped out. "You have us all. We'll keep you safe, little wolf."

The scent of honey hit his nose an instant before Kate's light touch was on his shoulder. She sniffled. His sweet mate, hurt by his loss. He leaned his face against her stomach, and she cradled his cheek as he stared down at Fina and cried for the first time since he'd buried Amelia.

Another hand rested on his back, and then another and another. He could smell them. He could *feel* them. The pack was piled on the bed behind him, mourning with him. His face crumpled, and he lifted Fina closer to his face, smelling her so he could become familiar with her scent, too, like he was with the rest of the pack. Because this was it, the moment everything changed. It was the moment everything became clear. There would be no more running from them or fighting their bond. There would be no more hiding far away from here and keeping them at a distance.

This was no longer a pack formed on a technicality.

This was the pack he and his wolf chose to bury themselves deeply within.

Fina had his fealty and so did the rest of them—Kate, Link, Chance, and Nicole.

This wasn't *the* pack anymore.

They were *his* pack.

THIRTEEN

Dalton was quiet as he drove back toward the main road that led to town. The moonlight was bright on his face as he rested an elbow on the open window and draped his other wrist over the steering wheel. There was no music, no joking, but it wasn't an uncomfortable silence.

Brave Dalton, holding Fina and facing down his demons. Kate didn't know how she knew it, but things would be different for him now. April First would be different. When she rested her hand on his leg, he cast her a smile. It wasn't the forced ones he'd given at dinner. This one said he was okay.

Seeing him break down like that had broken her apart inside. She'd walked in on him crying silently, staring at Fina. When the others came in, Nicole had cried right along with her, and even Link and Chance looked heartbroken. She already loved them all so much.

"Can we spend the night at the cabin?" she asked.

Dalton shot her a surprised look, hesitated a moment, then answered, "Yeah, sure."

"I want to have one night in there with you before you leave. Link offered to help me move my stuff into it this week if I wanted while you and Chance are at Silver Summit. I don't want to spend my first night there alone, though. I want my first night at our new place to be with you."

"About everything that happened tonight..."

He sounded apologetic, so she rushed out, "Tonight was perfect. I like them very much."

Dalton lifted her knuckles to his lips and let them linger. "I could tell they like you, too. I don't want to leave."

She raised his hand to her cheek and brushed against him. "I don't want you to either, but you love your job. It's good for your wolf to be out tracking in the wilderness. I can't keep you trapped here, Dalton. You'll wither, just like I would if you tried to stifle me. I have two days off in a row next week. I'll ask Ian or Tobias to fly me to you. I'm excited about seeing where you work. You have this entire side of your life that I don't know yet. And besides, I have a very busy week coming up."

Dalton took a left onto the now familiar turnoff for the cabin that would soon be theirs. "Oh, yeah?"

"I'm making cookies for all my neighbors in honor of warm weather. Little yellow frosted suns."

"Of course you are."

"And I'll be packing up and will be completely boring between that and work. You probably won't even think about me when you are in the bush with your bachelor clients, drinking beers, cooking out, fishing until your heart's content."

"False, I'm going to be one moody asshole out there. I may have to pick a fight with a grizzly just to sate my wolf. I know we'll have to get used to being apart like Jenner and Lena did, but adjusting will be hard."

"What time are you leaving tomorrow?"

"Jenner, Chance, and I are meeting Tobias at the runway outside of Galena at eight in the morning."

"At least you all get to carpool. Or planepool."

Dalton snorted at her terrible joke and pulled to a stop in front of the cabin. She met him at the front of the truck and followed him inside. It was as warm as she remembered, and the bed called to her weary bones, but when she pulled off her jacket, Dalton's eyes were steady and hungry on her in the moonlight that filtered through the big window. She giggled and prepared to tease him for his insatiable appetite, but he approached slowly and rested his hands so lightly on her waist she was stunned into silence. His lips were soft as he pressed them onto hers. Angling his head, he brushed his tongue past her lips. She opened for him, but where he usually worked into a frenzy, he ran his knuckles against her cheek and then turned her slowly in his hands until her back was to his chest.

The rustle of fabric sounded, and then his lips were on her neck, softly kneading her sensitive skin just under her ear as his fingertips brushed up under her sweater. He nipped gently at her skin, then eased away just long and far enough to pull her shirt over her head. And then his lips were there again, kissing, sucking, biting until she closed her eyes to the world and relaxed against him. His chest was bare and warm, and his hands glided easily up her ribcage and to her back, where he unsnapped her bra and pushed it from her arms in one smooth motion. As his hands cupped her breasts, she reached behind her head and gripped the back of his neck as he grazed his teeth on her earlobe.

"Dalton," she whispered.

He smiled against her skin and ran one of his hands down her stomach and into the front of her scrubs. She writhed against his palm as he slid one finger into her and then a second. He was stretching her, preparing her, but he wasn't rushing or losing control like he usually did. This was different than it had been between them. It was deeper, slower. He was revering her body with every stroke, every kiss.

With his free hand, he unsnapped his jeans and shucked his pants, and she did the same because she needed to feel his skin against hers.

The first stroke of his long shaft along her spine matched the one he gave her with his fingers, and she gasped at how good he felt. He wrapped his arm around her waist, pulling her against his erection as he pushed his fingers into her again. Her body tingled with a numbing warmth as he drove her closer to climax.

His arms shook as he rested his forehead against the back of her head and walked them slowly toward the bed. Kate thought he wanted to take her from behind, but he didn't. Instead, he turned her, cupped her cheeks, and drove his tongue against hers in a slow, sexy rhythm. Pulling her down with him, he sat on the bed as she straddled his lap and pulled her knees tight against his ribs.

When Dalton eased back, she could see it. His wolf was here in the blazing gold of his eyes, but so was Dalton. He was present in his adoring smile. Slowly, she slid over him until he was buried deep inside of her. She gasped his name when he touched her clit. Easing slowly upward, she hugged his shoulders tightly as his lips moved against hers. She was the sand, and he was gentle waves moving against her, and this was what it was all supposed to feel like. Love, safety, devotion.

He cupped his hand around the back of her neck and rolled them over until he was on top of her, never once separating their skin, never letting her go. "I love you so much," he whispered.

And she knew what he was feeling. She could almost taste his sadness. Could almost feel his desperation to stay near her every second he could before they were parted tomorrow. He moved within her, slowly, drawing out every stroke until she was lost on wave after wave of pleasure. His powerful stomach flexed against hers with every rock of his hips. And just when his body went rigid, he locked gazes with her. Unable to hold back anymore, orgasm pulsed through her body, each growing deeper until she gasped and arched back. Above her, Dalton pushed into her again and let off a soft, sexy huff of breath as his cock throbbed within her. Streams of wet heat shot into her, over and over, as Dalton jerked his hips. Then he closed his eyes.

And when the last of their aftershocks had faded away, he pulled the comforter over them and held her close, his thrumming pulse steady against her cheek as she drifted off into a beautiful, bottomless sleep, safe and warm in the arms of the man who held her heart.

FOURTEEN

"Hey, Kate, do you have a second?" Janice asked. "I really need to talk to you."

Kate frowned at the open door to room 101. She had a patient waiting on the release paperwork she held in her hands. He was newly stitched and bandaged after a nasty fall off a ladder where his arm had landed on a knife he'd been using to dig a nail out of rotted wooden siding. He was one of those grizzly mountain men who hated town and especially hated hospitals, and if she was being honest, she couldn't wait to get the grumpy old cuss out of here.

But Janice looked twitchy, and her voice had been tainted with worry.

"What's wrong?" Kate asked, approaching the check-in desk.

Janice shoved her glasses farther up her nose and cast a quick look around, then slid a folded piece of paper over the counter toward Kate. "Someone brought this for you."

Kate set her clipboard down and unfolded the letter.

Katherine Hawke,

You should leave. Leave here, leave Alaska. You're in way over your head. This isn't a threat. It's a warning.

Dread froze her in place as she read each terrifying word a second time. There was no signature, and she didn't recognize the handwriting. It was in all capital letters, dark ink scribbled onto the white paper like the author had stabbed each letter. She would blame Vega for this, but she saw his handwriting every day, and this wasn't it. Not even close.

"I read that," Janice said in a frightened whisper. "Kate, that sounds bad. What are you into, child?"

"Janice, who gave this to you?"

"A tall man came in here about fifteen minutes ago, looking around, real rangy. He was older, maybe in his fifties or early sixties, but built like a brick house. Silver hair, matching beard, but there was something strange about his face."

Leaning closer, Kate asked, "What was it?"

"Long scars down one cheek, like he'd been clawed by an animal. By a bear maybe."

Claw marks? She didn't know anyone who fit that description. Why would a complete stranger come in here and give her this ominous warning? She would've pretended this was meant for someone else if her danged name wasn't scribbled across that first line.

"Thanks, Janice," she said, troubled to her bones as she folded the paper and stuck it in the front pocket of her scrubs.

In a daze, she checked out her patient, had him sign his release forms, told him what to look for and how to care for his wound, then advised him to use a suitable tool, not a knife, on nails in the future. He'd grumbled his thanks and escaped the room before she could even put the paperwork back in order.

She missed Dalton. There it was. If he was here, he would know what to do with this stupid note and hug her and make her feel safe again. But he was out guiding a tour, and even if he called her from a satellite phone, was it fair of her to tell him about the note? What could he do about it from the wilderness except worry about her? He'd had enough trouble saying goodbye when she'd gone with him to the airstrip outside of Galena. Tobias Silver had grown impatient with how long Dalton had stalled loading up, and this note wasn't going to help his protective instincts at all.

Lost in the sea of her churning thoughts, she turned in her paperwork to Janice and made her way into the supply room to grab clean sheets and hand sanitizer to refill the empty dispenser on the wall of room 101.

The door opened and closed behind her, and Kate smiled to herself. Lacy always snuck in here after her to gossip when she had a break between patients.

"Did you get a love note from your pet monster?" Dr. Vega asked, his voice edged with fury.

"That's none of your business," she said, turning slowly. She put the folded sheets in front of her like a shield.

"See, that's where you're wrong. Dalton is my business."

"No, he's really not, and this is completely inappropriate behavior, Dr. Vega. You can't keep approaching me like this." She made to leave, but he stepped in front of the door. His dark eyes looked insane right now, and he'd shaved his thinning hair off completely, making him look more intimidating somehow. "Move."

"Not until you listen to reason." He reached forward as if he was going to stroke her cheek, and she flinched away from him. "Pretty angel, fallen from heaven to play with demons. You remind me of my daughter sometimes, Kate. She's about your age. Pretty, good head on her shoulders. She's smart, though. Smarter than you." His voice had gone dreamy, and this was the first she'd ever even heard of his daughter. "Doesn't it bother you that you are nothing to them? You're collateral damage. A womb. Your boyfriend isn't here anymore, is he?"

"I don't know what you're talking about."

"Yes, you do! He's gone off to Silver Summit, leaving you unprotected. You aren't one of them. He tainted you and left you here, and now I can't fucking stand to look at you. All I want is to work in peace, but you're here reminding me of them. You're such a *disappointment*."

Fear pounded through her veins with every beat of her heart, and she sidled along the wall as he approached with slow, calculated steps.

She was trapped in here with a psychopath!

"Lacy!" she screamed. "Janice!"

"Oh," he said, frowning. "Don't taint them, too."

With a screech, she threw the sheets at his face and bolted for the door. Just as her hand landed on the knob, Dr. Vega jerked her back by the arm, and in desperation to escape, she reared back and slapped him across the face.

There was a moment of stunned silence, and she used it. She twisted the knob and bolted out into the hallway.

Janice was already running toward her, panic in her eyes. "What's happened?"

"Nothing," Dr. Vega said, his cheek red from her palm as he came out of the supply room looking completely calm. "She's just feeling hysterical right now."

Kate was pressed against the opposite wall of the hallway. Her entire body shook relentlessly as she heaved breath.

"Kate?" Janice asked. Her face said she didn't believe a word Dr. Vega had said.

Kate's voice was gone. Her throat tightened around her words, forcing them back down as she struggled for breath and made her way down the wall, farther away from Dr. Vega.

"What did you do to her?" Janice yelled.

"He grabbed me," Kate choked out. "I want to report him."

"Hell yeah, we're reporting this shit," Janice gritted out, grabbing her wrist. "You've lost your mind, Dr. Vega. We've put up with a lot over the years, but you won't get away with this."

"Kate," Dr. Vega called. "Kate! Think about what you're doing. I hold all the cards. I have the power! Me! Kate!" His shoes squeaked across the tile floors behind them. "She slapped me, Janice. She slapped my face. She attacked me. I'm going to report you, Kate. You stupid, fucking, traitor bitch. I'm going to report you! You'll be fired for what you did to me!"

"Don't listen to him," Janice said, tugging Kate behind the check-in desk. She punched a trio of numbers on the phone and said, "Don't you come another step, you old fool. You're in deep enough. I'm calling the police."

Dr. Vega was still coming, so Kate lurched forward and pulled out the pocket knife she kept in her purse. "Don't you come another step closer. I mean it."

Dr. Vega paced in front of the counter, and now two patients were peeking out of their rooms. Lacy was trying to usher them back inside, and when Dr. Vega started walking toward her, she ran inside room 102 with a patient and closed the door.

Yelling a terrifying sound of pure rage, Dr. Vega tried to pry the door open.

"Lacy, don't let him in!" Kate screamed.

Janice was talking low into the phone, telling the dispatcher what was happening. With a look of pure, red-faced fury, Dr. Vega strode back toward them and took a stack of clipboards off the counter, then chucked them at Kate. She took a metal clip edge in the temple and cried out as she stumbled backward. But when her vision cleared, Dr. Vega was running out of the front exit.

Janice shot Kate a terrified look, but she didn't stop murmuring her account of what was happening into the phone.

Sirens sounded in the distance, and Lacy was suddenly there, murmuring words that made no sense as she probed Kate's throbbing temple. Kate's cheek was warm, and stunned, she dragged her gaze from the exit where Dr. Vega had disappeared to the white tile beneath her. Drops of red made tiny splat sounds right beside her sneakers.

Dalton wasn't the monster.

Dr. Vega was.

FIFTEEN

Kate hated moving. Oh sure, she was beyond excited to be in the cabin, but the actual act of moving was a pain in the butt. Add to that three stitches for the cut in her hairline and pain medicine that made her a little groggy, and today wasn't her favorite.

"Is anyone else coming to help?" Nicole asked as she patted down another strip of masking tape over a full box.

"No. I asked Avril to come, but she declined the invite."

"Your sister?"

"Yeah. Her husband helped me when I moved into this place, and I thought I could take them out to dinner after we were done. It would be a good excuse to spend some time together, but when I told Avril about moving in with Dalton, she called this 'just another bad decision in a string of many.'"

"Geez," Nicole muttered. "She sounds charming."

Fina twitched in her sleep in the portable swing, and they both went still and quiet, waiting for her to wake up. When she didn't, Nicole grabbed a marker and wrote *Kitchen* on the box.

"Thank goodness for you and Link," Kate said, feeling emotional. "I would be doing this all by myself if you hadn't offered to help."

Link was a quiet sort of man, but from the kitchen where he was wrapping plates in thick moving paper, he said, "We're glad to help. It's not every day we get a new pack member, and you are doing more for us than you know."

Kate lowered a heavily wrapped flower vase into a box. "What do you mean?"

Link gave her a look over his shoulder. His eyes were so light gray it had been unsettling at first, but now she was growing used to him.

"I mean you're giving my wolves a reason to come home."

She dipped her gaze shyly as warmth flooded her cheeks. It was nice to feel a little needed.

"This wasn't much of a pack before you came along," Nicole admitted.

"Dalton told me he kept himself distanced."

"Yeah, but packs are tricky. One unhappy wolf, and everyone feels it. Deeply. I think Chance wanted us all to be closer like Link did, but Dalton was hurting and kept everyone separate."

"It feels right now," Link said, his back to them as though he was talking more to himself.

"It does to me, too," Nicole said, her marked cheek stretching with a grin. "Plus now I'm not the only human."

Kate took the tape Nicole offered and fiddled with the sticky edge. "Sometimes this all feels so fast. I mean, when I'm with Dalton, I feel so certain. There is no hesitation, no fear. But he's been gone almost a week now, and every day he's away, these stupid little insecurities creep in."

"Like what?"

"Like am I rushing this? I was really hurt by my ex, and then by Miller. My boss is being horrible to me about my relationship with Dalton, and my sister thinks every decision I make is wrong. I keep thinking maybe I'm desperate for someone to love me properly, you know? But then I close my eyes and think of how I feel around Dalton, and then I think my insecurities are stupid because he's everything I could've ever dreamed of in a man. In a partner. In a best friend. It's this vicious loop, over and over, making me second-guess everything."

"Kate, that's not stupid. That's natural. It's different for Link and Dalton. Hell, it'll be different for Chance if he ever settles down with a human. But for us, we're not only humans, we're women. We feel deeply, analyze everything, and when our mates aren't around to remind us how loved we are, it's easy to slip into old insecurities."

Link pulled a box off the counter and set it on the floor by the front door. "For you it feels fast, but I assure you, for Dalton, time is dragging. Our animals have a lot of say in the decisions we make. Maybe if Dalton was human, he would need months, even years, to decide if you're the one he wants. But it's not like that for werewolves. For any shifters, really. The animal can see you. Can sense the good in you. Can tell you're compatible almost immediately. It was the same for me. I obsessed over Nicole, brought her fish and dead rabbits as gifts while I was a wolf, but she didn't understand my need to be around her and to take care of her. I could see it was confusing for her, even scared her sometimes, but I was driven to keep doing it, anyway."

"Dead rabbits?"

Nicole laughed and nodded. "I didn't know werewolves existed yet, I had just moved to Alaska, and I had this massive wolf bringing me dead things. I thought he was trying to lure me outside to eat me."

Kate giggled and settled onto her folded legs. "This makes me feel better. I was starting to think Dalton and I had both gone insane."

"Uuuh, Dalton *has* gone insane. Do you know how many times he's called us?" Nicole's dark eyebrow arched up. "Ten times, at least, and from a damned satellite phone, just asking for us to check on you. That fight with Dr. Vega has him worried something fierce. He made Link drive out to the medical center during one of your shifts just to make sure that asshole doctor wasn't giving you grief. Dalton hates being away from you like this."

"Well, Dr. Vega spent most of the week in the police station. He didn't pass a sobriety test, and he was full of death threats. He sobered up enough not to land in the psych ward in Anchorage, but from what I hear, it was a close call. He's not allowed within a hundred yards of me, and he was officially fired from the medical center this morning for misconduct. He won't bother me anymore." She wished she felt as confident as she sounded. She was still pretty shaken by his whole tirade. Janice and Lacy were too. "Dalton was right. Something is really wrong with Dr. Vega." She almost pitied the man. That considerable amount of hate must weigh heavily on him. What a sad and empty life.

Nicole gave Link a loaded look, and a million things passed between them in an instant.

"What?" Kate asked.

"You should be careful around him," Link said. "It's a small town, and at some point you'll cross paths. Don't provoke him, don't even talk to him if you can avoid it. Over the last year, I've found several traps on our land. Big ones. I confronted the owner of the trap line, who is trespassing, but each time he seems less and less apologetic."

Horrified by the idea of one of the wolves getting stuck in one, she asked, "Who's setting the traps?"

"Emanuel Vega."

The blood drained from her face, leaving her skin cold and tingly. "Oh my gosh, Link. He really knows, doesn't he?"

Link squatted down beside her and Nicole and forced a smile. "We'll figure everything out. It's not the first time in our history we've dealt with disgruntled humans. Let me worry about Vega. Today is a good day."

With a shaky sigh, she nodded. "If there is anything I can do, you'll let me know?"

"Of course. What I mostly need you to do is be wary and safe around him, though. He's dangerous."

"But I don't understand why he's so angry. You are members of the community. You help people. Everyone in town knows if they need construction work, you're the man to do the job, and you charge fairly. You stay under the radar."

Link let off a dark laugh. "Well, my family didn't care so much about staying hidden. I'm starting to get the feeling their bad decisions are haunting us. We'll figure it all out, though."

Kate's phone rang, and butterflies fluttered around her stomach as she recognized the number. It wasn't the satellite phone Dalton had been using to keep in touch while he was out in the bush, but his cell phone number instead.

"Hi," she answered breathlessly.

"Hey, beautiful," he greeted in that deep, sexy voice of his. "How is moving day going?"

Besides the news about Vega the pecker-face werewolf trapper? "It's going okay. We're about done boxing everything up. It'll take a few trips because I can't get my truck to start and all we have is Link's Bronco, but we should get it done by tonight."

"I wish I could be there."

"Me, too. I miss you! And I need your muscles."

Dalton's chuckle made her close her eyes at how good his laugh sounded over the line. It had been an eternal week without him.

"Well, I have a surprise for you. A delivery."

"A delivery of what?"

"Of muscles." A knock sounded at the door.

Hope unfurled inside her, and she stood, then padded to the front door. With one baffled glance over her shoulder at Link and Nicole, who were grinning knowingly, she opened the door.

Dalton stood there, looking like a tall glass of water in a scorching desert. Long, powerful legs splayed, muscular chest and shoulders pressing against the thin fabric of a blue sweater, the top two buttons of which were undone to expose that sexy crease between his pecs. A dark beard covered the bottom half of his face, and his eyes were lightened to a caramel brown that danced and sparked as he smiled down at her. Slowly, he lowered the phone from his ear.

"Dalton!" Kate jumped and clung, wrapping her legs around his waist as she kissed him. His beard was sexy as heck, but it prickled her and made her laugh as he pulled her closer and thrust his tongue past her lips. Dalton, Dalton, Dalton, her Dalton. She'd missed him so much, and he was here. Here! "You beastly bearded man, you're tickling me!"

Dalton rubbed his cheek against hers roughly and laughed unapologetically. When he settled her on her feet, he was grinning big, and his eyes were the color of evening sunlight. Brawny, beautiful, fearsome Alaskan werewolf, and he was hers.

"What are you doing here? I thought you were still on the fishing tour."

"The tour ended this morning, and I busted my ass unpacking us, taking care of the horses, and restocking the woodpile. I had to get chores done, but I'd asked Tobias to come pick me up so I could try and make it in time to move you. I hated thinking about you doing this without me." His gaze landed on her temple, and the smile dropped from his lips in an instant. "Shit, Kate," he murmured, running a light fingertip just under her stitches. "You said it was nothing but a scrape."

"I don't want to talk about Dr. Vega." *Ever again.* "I want to forget about him and move on." Overcome with emotion, she hugged him tight and buried her face against his chest. Every ounce of uncertainty had trickled from her body the second she'd kissed him. Finally, after the everlasting week she'd had, she felt safe again.

Dalton cupped her head, hugging her tightly. She could feel his words just as well as hear them. "Don't go to pieces on me, woman. I need to introduce you to some people."

She looked up at him. "What?"

Dalton leaned down slowly, sipped her lips, then jerked his head to the side. "We're going to get your things in one trip." He turned her slowly, moving so that his wide shoulders didn't block the street anymore. Up the stairs behind him, Chance grinned at her through a scruffy blond beard, and just behind him stood a couple of giant, familiar men, one tiny, golden-eyed woman, and Elyse and Lena. The Silvers.

"Hey, Kate," Ian said, his bright blue eyes dancing as he shook her hand. "It's good to see you again."

"Hi," she said, stunned as Chance gave her a quick hug in passing.

Tobias climbed down the stairs toward her and offered his hand for a shake, too.

Oh, she'd known them before this because Galena was a small town and everyone knew everyone, but this was her first time seeing them since she'd found out they hid freaking grizzly bears inside of them.

One by one, the Silvers trickled into her tiny apartment. Elyse gave her a back-cracking hug with one arm, holding her baby boy with the other. Lena followed suit and told her "Welcome to the family."

The last Silver mate stopped in front of her, head canted as she studied Kate. "I'm Vera Silver," the golden-eyed woman said, offering her hand.

"I'm Kate Hawke," she said, feeling breathless. "You saved Link. You saved Fina." She didn't mean to fan-girl out on her, but, well, there it was. Vera was good and was working to help shifters in ways no one had been able to do in history. Pursing her lips in embarrassment, Kate forced herself to stop shaking Vera's hand.

"I made you beer and beef jerky, and I'm going to save your girl babies. We're going to be friends."

"Okay," Kate said on a stunned breath as Vera pulled her into an organ-squishing hug.

"Accept my affection," Vera whispered.

"I wouldn't fight it," Dalton teased from beside them. "She's relentless. Her time on Perl Island made her a clingy weirdo."

Vera snapped her teeth at Dalton. "Accept it," she repeated to Kate.

Feeling a little like she was in a dream, Kate lifted her arms and hugged Vera back, hard, who then released Kate to go greet Link inside. Vera examined Link's eyes immediately, pulling his cheeks down, one and then the other, while he ruffled her chestnut curls. And when she seemed satisfied, she hugged Link up tight. She hooked arms with Nicole, then headed straight for Fina as the others greeted Link with low murmurs and chuckles. Her apartment was filled with happy reunions and laughter, and she couldn't help the smile that stretched her face.

Her sister and brother-in-law might not have come through, but these almost strangers were now picking up boxes stacked three high as if they weighed no more than a rung of computer paper, smiles on their faces as if they were happy to be here.

"You look emotional again," Dalton said, hugging her tight to his side.

"I'm not," she lied.

He swept her off her feet so fast her stomach dipped, then climbed up the stairs to the yard. The snow was completely gone now, and little shoots of green grass poked up everywhere as the midday sun beamed down. It was warm enough that she wasn't even freezing without her jacket on.

"Where are you taking me?" she asked. She should really be helping the others.

"Your truck. We need to pull it around to load."

"It's not working. The engine won't turn over. I have to take it into the shop."

Without missing a step, Dalton settled her on her feet and pressed his lips to hers, backing her toward the old blue Ford sitting underneath the awning beside her landlord's car. "I'll get you both running," he promised between kisses.

Warmth dumped in her middle, and she could feel her heartbeat between her legs, pounding with need. "You know about cars?" she gasped as his lips plucked at the sensitive skin of her neck.

"I do." He backed her to the front of the Ford and popped the hood with one hand, successfully blocking them from the road.

"We can't do this here," she said. The Silvers were already loading up, walking back and forth to their trucks that lined the curb out front. She could hear them talking and joking!

"*We* won't. You will." Dalton pressed against her, pinning her to the grill of her truck as he ground his erection against her. "Fuck, woman, I've missed you. It was torture being out there with a bunch of dudes, and thinking about you. Thinking about the things we've done together." He slipped his hand down the front of her jeans and pressed his finger inside of her as she rocked against his palm. "All I wanted to do was come home and hold you. Come home and feel this." He dragged his fingertip through her wet heat, then slid into her again. "I wanted to come home and feel you come for me."

The pressure was already blinding. Too fast. She was already there. To stifle her moan, she clamped her teeth hard on his chest. A soft snarl, one she'd missed indescribably much, rattled from him as he pushed his finger into her again and again. Her orgasm blasted through her in deep, quick pulses, and Dalton slowed his rhythm as she clutched his sweater.

Breath ragged, she released his skin from her bite and went limp against him. Dalton cupped her neck, just beneath her ear, and kissed her gently, but the stony erection pressed against her belly said he was still thoroughly worked up. Dalton smiled against her lips, nipped her once, then leveled her with those sexy, golden eyes. "Next time you bite me, you better mean it."

"Bloodthirsty," she accused in a weak voice.

Dalton slid his hand out of her jeans and hugged her close, his warm body pressed against every inch of hers. With a wicked grin, he murmured, "Not bloodthirsty. I want your mark. Now, go try to start the truck. I need to hear how it sounds when the engine tries to turn over."

Boneless, she stumbled this way and that like a noodle until she pulled the door open and scrambled inside the cab of her truck. She turned the engine. It stuttered for a while, but never caught. She leaned out the door to watch Dalton as she tried again.

He was standing with his arms locked on the frame, frowning as he looked at the innards of her ride.

"Hold up," he said, then began unplugging and checking things she had no guess at. He glared at the end of a line, blew on it, then plugged it in again, muttering to himself. He pushed and pulled, and at last said, "You need a new belt soon. This one's cracked to hell and won't last much longer, but she'll hold for today."

"Is that what's wrong with it?"

"No, that doesn't have anything to do with it not starting. Try again."

She twisted the key, and the engine stuttered and almost caught this time.

"Again," he said, gripping the frame as he stared inside.

She turned the key, and this time it caught and held. Holy moly, Dalton was a sexpot. She hadn't known he was so good with cars, but thinking about it, she wasn't surprised. Any time she complained about something not working in her apartment, he'd fixed it within a day.

His hands were covered in oil, but he didn't seem to mind one bit as he closed the hood and said, "Go ahead and back her up to the edge of the driveway so we don't have to walk so far. She'll start again, but I need to pick up a few parts before I head back to Silver Summit."

Talk of him leaving so soon had her heart dipping to her toes. She swiveled in the seat to face the open door. "When are you going?"

"Tomorrow," he said, settling between her legs as she sat on the driver's seat with the rumble of the idling engine filling the air.

"Nooo. I just got you back."

"Black bear season starts next week, and we always get pummeled with tours when they come out of hibernation."

She knew all about bears from growing up in bear country. "That sounds dangerous. They're hungry and angry when they wake up."

Dalton leaned forward and sucked on her bottom lip playfully, then lowered his kisses to her neck. "Are you worried for me, mate?"

"Heck yes, I am. I never really thought about what you do before you mentioned hunting freaking bears."

"Aaah, but if you saw my wolf, you wouldn't worry so much."

"Maybe you should show me him before you leave then, because now I'm going to be dreaming of bears attacking you."

Dalton froze, then eased away from her, his eyes gone deadly serious. "Kate, my animal isn't like wild wolves. I want you to see him, but you still smell like fear half the time I growl."

"I do?"

"Faintly, but yeah. Your adrenaline still kicks in. You told me you have nightmares about seeing Miller Change. I don't want your nightmares associated with me. I want to show you that part of myself when you're ready."

She gripped his sweater and sighed. She didn't like this—him hiding part of himself—but she understood. Miller's Change had been awful. Bones breaking, snapping so loud it sounded like gunfire out in her backyard, and his body had contorted and reshaped as she'd watched in horror. His wolf had been terrifying, with white eyes and bared teeth, and he'd turned on the door, scratching and clawing, trying to get to her before he gave up and left. Everything in her that night had told her Miller would've killed her if that door hadn't been in the way. The sight of him had filled her with a fear greater than she'd ever known, and Dalton was trying to protect her from being scared like that again.

Knowing what he was and seeing what he was were two totally different things.

"Hey, do you have a couple days you can take off in a row?"

"Why?" she asked cheekily.

"Because I want you to come out on one of my tours. I talked to Lennard and Jenner, and they said they can always use your nursing skills, just in case. They said you're welcome on any tour. Lena goes on some of Jenner's as their photographer, but I wanted to make sure before I asked you."

She beamed. "Really? Will I get to ride a horse? I love horses. Can I fish? I don't have any fish in my freezer. I have a license. Will we sleep in a tent? Can you see the northern lights better out on Kodiak?"

Dalton looked utterly amused as he nodded at each of her rattled-off questions. "Yes, yes, yes, all of it. I'll give you a list Lennard gives all our clients on what to pack. He's excited about meeting you. He was convinced I'd never settle down."

"Your boss is a lot nicer than mine was."

"Lennard's more than a boss. He's like a father figure."

She frowned. "Dalton, you never talked about your dad."

"He's the one who taught me about cars," he said with a sad smile. "Chance used to spend a week at a time at our homestead. We were both only children, so our families passed us back and forth together so we had another pup to grow up with. Chance can fix just about anything, too, because of my dad. He looked Ute, like I do."

"Looked." Past tense.

"He was shot. Hunted. He was a wolf at the time. Alaska can be a sanctuary for us because we can run wild in a landscape where it's natural to see wolves. It can also be a curse."

"Because of wolf hunts."

Dalton nodded solemnly.

"I'm so sorry, Dalton."

"It was a long time ago. I was thirteen when he passed, and Chance's dad helped raise me when I needed a man in my life. When I started my Changes at sixteen, I had guidance. Chance and I both did. We were luckier than most. The Silvers' dad, Clayton, didn't tell them anything about their Changes, didn't tell them anything about hibernation, and they almost died that first winter."

"Dalton!" Vera called. "Cease humping. The trucks are almost loaded up."

"Already?" Kate asked, shocked.

Dalton kissed her one last time, tickling her with his beard.

"You need a shave."

"I don't bring a razor on tours. You don't like it?"

"It's sexy as frick, but it'll rub me raw."

"Sexy as frick," he repeated, his eyes on her lips. "Someday you'll say what you mean."

"You want my mouth filthy like yours," she accused.

His smile looked downright predatory as he nodded.

He turned away, but she grabbed his hand. "Dalton?"

"Hmm?"

She dipped her voice to a whisper. "You look sexy as fuck."

His lips were on her in a blur, rough teeth grazing her lips. He gripped her hair tightly and dragged in a ragged breath as he pressed his hips between her legs.

"Dalton!" Vera barked out, closer this time. "I said cease humping, not hump more!"

He growled and released Kate reluctantly. His eyes couldn't pass for human at all right now as he adjusted his erection and gave her one last naughty look before he turned and strode away.

Feeling utterly drunk on Dalton, she pressed her fingertips across her throbbing lips.

And as she watched him walk away with those sexy, confident strides, she couldn't remember a single reason why she hadn't liked cursing before.

SIXTEEN

"Do you like them?" Dalton asked, trying to keep his voice nonchalant, like her answer didn't mean the whole entire world to him.

"The Silvers? I love them all. They're funny and loud, and they made sure to include me in everything tonight, just like the pack did. I'm glad everyone stayed to cut loose. And I'm double glad Vera brought booze because we are fresh out of everything here." Kate relaxed against his chest and stared at the full moon outside the giant window behind their bed. She sat between his legs, her soft red hair draped over his shoulder. With a sigh, she hugged his arms around her chest tighter. He wished they could stay just like this forever.

He kissed her temple and inhaled her scent, closing his eyes to revel in it. He'd imagined it a million times this past week, but nothing could touch the real thing. "Tell me about growing up a Hawke."

Kate brushed her soft cheek against his forearm, and there was a smile in her voice when she said, "Every day was the same. Wake up, feed the dogs, then get myself ready. Always the dogs first. I got jealous for a couple of years because the dogs were my parents' entire life. Their entire focus. But then they let me keep one of the puppies. She was red and white and a submissive runt that never strengthened for dog sledding. She couldn't hear out of one of her ears, so they let me have her. She was the first dog we had inside. The others were work dogs that needed to stay used to the weather, but Sasha slept with me every night. Followed me around when I rode our four-wheeler, tried to steal fish anytime I was feeding the others. She was a little terror as a puppy, but I trained her myself. Even half deaf, she was smart. And little by little, I got it. I understood how my parents felt about their dogs. I started noticing their faces when they sold a dog. Sadness mixed with pride because that dog was bred and trained to make a good sled dog. They were driven to make Hawke Huskies the premier name in Iditarod dogs, and they did. It was admirable." She angled her head. "At least later I admired them when I was done sulking about losing attention to the barkers. My sister is two years older, and she purchased her first dogs from my parents' line as soon as she moved out. And they were so proud of her. She married young, built on the family name, and they had that same look in their eyes when Avril would leave from family dinners or holiday get-togethers. Sadness that she was leaving. Pride that she'd made something of herself."

"And you?"

"They didn't understand me. I wanted to go to college in Anchorage and work toward a career. I wanted to be a nurse, but they were upset that I was taking out school loans when they'd practically handed me a profession that I could make a living at. I resented them. I saw the way they looked at Avril, and with each year I was in school, there was less and less pride in me and more and more sadness for my decisions. I felt like they didn't value what I was doing, the hard work I was putting in. It hurt being the least favorite, and eventually my sister and her husband began spending a lot of time with my parents where I wasn't invited. I felt forgotten."

Dalton hugged her closer. The smile had gone from her voice, and now it was raw and quiet.

"Is that why you take care of other people?"

"I don't do that much," she murmured. "Not enough."

"The first time I met you, you were in that bar facing down that asshole in pool to win back a neighbor's rent money. You were wearing scrubs in that bar, sticking out like a sore thumb, and you smelled tired. Tired and scared. I thought you were some shark. Pretending to be submissive maybe. A con artist. And I followed to see you return the money and give your neighbor whiskey for her aches, at the expense of Darren hurting you. You were fearless for the people you cared about. That's when I knew."

Kate turned in his arms, her eyes so big and green in the moonlight. "When you knew what?"

"That I wanted you. Needed you. I tried to push it off as desperation to escape April First, but it wasn't. It was just you." He sipped her small lips and brushed her mussed hair off her cheek. Damn he loved the way she looked after they slept together. Flushed and disheveled. So beautiful. "Why are you wanting to start breeding sled dogs now?" He wanted to make sure it was for the right reasons, and not as some desperate move to make her parents proud. They should've been proud of what she'd accomplished already, and he hated the thought of her grasping at approval for the rest of her life.

"I've done nursing for several years now, and I'm good at it. I'm confident with my job, and I like helping people. But for the last couple of years, I keep thinking of Sasha. I keep thinking how good I felt when I turned her from an unmanageable puppy to a well-behaved dog. She would get so proud of herself, you know? I could see it. I don't want to have a huge operation like my parents or my sister. I'm not interested in the family business. I'm interested in the dogs. Even more so now that I've met you."

"What do you mean?"

"Pack dynamics. I understand them better because of the time I spent with dog teams. Their hierarchy, the posturing, picking the personalities that would work best for a team. I'm more interested now than ever."

"Have you told your parents yet?"

"No. I know it sounds strange, but I don't want them knowing until they have to. I don't want them crowing about how they were right all along, or bringing up the time I wasted in school, or the money I wasted paying back all those student loans. I don't want to quit nursing completely, not for a while, and I wouldn't change anything about my journey here. They wouldn't understand though, you know?"

He rasped his beard against her cheek and rested his chin on her shoulder. "Yeah. I get that."

"And I know they would expect me to use the family name and the same bloodlines, but I don't think I want to do that either. I want to build up my own name. A different one."

Awed, Dalton rocked her gently and watched the swaying evergreen trees outside. She wasn't even going to use her parents' name in an effort to build from the ground up. Maybe her parents had picked a favorite kid, but that hadn't bowed Kate. It had made her lock her legs and stand strong instead. It gave her motivation to live her own life outside of the shadow her parents had created. She didn't see it, but Dalton did. Avril would always be a branch of her parents' business, never the main trunk. Kate was growing her own tree, and someday, it would have the potential to eclipse them all.

"We could call it Dawson Huskies," he murmured, testing the waters. Because if he was honest, he wanted his ring on her finger now. He wanted her to be a wolf bride. He wanted his last name on her as soon as she was ready to say yes, but Link had advised him to take things at her pace.

She clamped her teeth gently on his forearm. "Don't tease me."

"I'm not. I wouldn't tease about that."

"What are you saying?"

Dalton took a long steadying breath and used his words from the first time he'd admitted he loved her. "You know what I'm about to ask you, don't you?"

"I hope so," she answered on a breath.

"Wait here." He climbed off the bed, his heart hammering against his ribs as he dug through his pack he brought back with him. The velvet pouch was soft against his calloused fingertips as he pulled it from the front pocket. The gold strings were worn where he'd opened it a hundred times over the last week, just to look at the ring and imagine how this moment would go. *Please say yes.*

When he upended the pouch, the single diamond on the ring glinted in the blue moonlight. He turned and approached her slowly, but she was on the edge of the bed now, hands clasped over her mouth, her eyes full as she looked at the ring he held up.

Dropping down to his knees in front of her, he leaned his forearms against the mattress, between her knees. "Kate, I love you. I know what I want, and it's you. Coming back to you was the best feeling in the world." He rolled his gaze over the rafters above them. "Coming back to this place, knowing it'll be ours, was such a huge deal for me. But this place wasn't a home until you decided to make it one with me. I want it all. I didn't know I could have this life, didn't know if I could be any good at it, but you make me feel like I can be better. Like if I work hard enough, maybe I can make you as happy as you make me. I want a life with you— dogs, babies, sunshine cookies for the neighbors, warm summers, cold winters, and cabin fever right along with you. I want everything. With you. But this is your decision. This is where you tell me what you want, and either way, I'll still be here, I'll still love you." He let off a shaky, nervous breath. "Kate, do you want to be my wife?"

Her face crumbled, and she leaned forward with a soft sob as her shoulders shook with emotion. So gently, she rested her forehead on his shoulder and nodded.

"Yes?" he asked, chest feeling like it would implode with the weight of uncertainty.

"Yes," she squeaked out.

The warmth of her tears spilled on and on as he held her, rocking her slowly.

His beautiful mate, so sensitive and soft and perfect.

It was minutes before her shoulders stopped shaking completely, but at last, she eased back just enough to hold her hand out for him to slip the ring on. She looked at the glinting diamond for a moment, then melted against him again, arms tight around his neck as she whispered, "I want all of that, too, Dalton. I want you."

"You're sure?" he asked, too afraid to hope she was really saying yes to everything.

She smiled, her pretty green eyes so full of emotion. "In all my life, I've never been so sure of anything." Wiping her damp cheeks with the back of her hand, Kate whispered, "Dalton Dawson, you and I just fit."

She drew his palm to her lips and kissed him just on the curve that connected his thumb to his wrist. She bit down gently, and Dalton let off a long breath. Sexy mate was going to get herself covered again if she wasn't careful.

"Remember when you told me the next time I bite you, I better mean it?"

Dalton froze as she turned and pulled her sleep shirt over her head, revealing that hot little evergreen tattoo on her ribs. She turned slowly until the light glinted off the shiny pink claiming mark Miller had given her.

Kate smelled like fear now, but she held his gaze bravely over her shoulder. "Mean it," she whispered.

This was happening. Dalton ran a light touch over the mark, put there without her consent, without her knowing what it meant. Now she knew exactly what it meant. She knew how it would bind them, and she wanted it. Wanted him. She wore his ring and called herself his mate, and it would've been enough for him. But she was gifting him more. Kate was giving him all of herself.

"It'll hurt," he warned as she settled on her hands and knees, perfect ass pointed at him.

"I remember."

Swallowing a growl for Miller, he climbed over her and rocked her forward gently, testing her arm strength. Testing how much of his weight she could bear without buckling. The curve of her back was soft and sloping under his light touch, and she arched her back, presenting for him. His mouth watered at the thought of tasting her blood. He was a monster with beastly thoughts, and she should know what she was binding herself to.

"I want to do this. My teeth are getting sharper just thinking about sinking them into your skin. You should see the beast in me before we do this. It's big. Bigger than marriage. My wolf will be yours for always if I do this, Kate."

She rocked back against him and pulled her hair aside, down one shoulder so he could see all of her back. "You aren't a beast," she said in a husky voice. "You're a wolf, and you don't scare me."

"You smell like fear."

"And what else?"

He inhaled deeply as he pushed his dick into her slowly. So tight. Fuck, he loved the feel of her around him. "Excitement." Running his hand up her back, he reveled in the softness of her muscles there. No tension. "You feel relaxed."

"Because I'm ready."

She swayed with him as he eased out and then pushed into her again. God, he loved her. Loved this. So wet. Wet for him because she loved him. Loved him touching her. He'd felt unlovable, untouchable, repulsive after Shelby. He'd been so scared of letting someone else hurt him like that, but Kate had thawed his frozen heart and brought him back to life. His beautiful mate deserved his bite, the protection of his body, his devotion, his pledge to be her partner in all things.

He reached around and cupped her sex, pressed gently on her clit as he slid into her again. A sexy little gasp left her lips as she arched her back for him again. His hips jerked. Losing control. Needed to stay gentle. *Take care with our mate.* Squeezing his eyes closed, he pressed into her again. Couldn't slow down now. Almost there. Too much pressure, too fast. Bucking. So tight. He slammed into her harder, and she was panting his name now. God, he loved the word on her lips. She yelled as the first pulse of her orgasm squeezed him. Now. He pressed his lips against Miller's mark. Not his anymore. Not after tonight. *Bite her! Make her ours!*

Dalton snarled and sank his teeth into her. He thrust into her and froze, dick throbbing as he spilled into her. She didn't make a sound as the taste of iron touched his tongue.

He didn't want to hurt her. Didn't want it, but if he didn't bite deep enough it wouldn't cover Miller's mark. Fucking Miller. He wished he could kill him twice for hurting Kate. For hurting his. *Ours.*

Kate was rigid under him as he emptied into her. Releasing her torn skin, he ran his tongue over her new claiming mark, reveling in the taste of her skin, her flesh, her blood. Mine.

His chest heaved as he eased back, rocking gently to match her aftershocks. He'd cleaned it well, but his bite was a ring of red, and a trickle of crimson dripped down her ribs. Pain. Blood. This was the cost of mating with a man like him.

Not a beast, though. A wolf. She absolved us. She sees us. Loves us.

Guilt mingled with relief as he ran his tongue up her ribs and cleaned her again. Her arms shook under her, and she lurched forward onto her elbows. She didn't smell like fear anymore, but still, he was afraid to look in her eyes when she cast him a glance over her shoulder. He kept his gaze on the bite he'd given. Shame. Fuck. He was so damned happy to see her cut from his teeth, but there was shame there, too. If she'd met a normal guy, she wouldn't hurt like this. She wouldn't bleed for tradition. She wouldn't be in pain to settle his possessive instincts.

With a long sigh, Kate turned, breaking their connection, then straddled his lap. She cupped his cheeks and lifted his gaze.

Her smile faltered, and she looked so damned proud. He didn't understand as she ran her fingertip under his eye. "My wolf. My man," she whispered. "Are you ready?"

"Ready for what?"

"It's your turn."

He caught what she meant an instant before she lowered her lips to his chest. Hugging her tight, encouraging her, he gritted his teeth. "Mean it."

Pain. Biting pain burning through him like fire in his veins. Tendrils of ache spread from her bite, reaching his limbs and burning through his fingertips. He wrapped his arm around her back and pulled her tighter against him as a long growl rattled his chest.

She didn't clean him like he'd done for her, but he understood. She was human. Good. Blood wasn't her taste, but when she eased back, her lips were red, and she was crying again. Warmth ran down his chest, and he anchored himself in this moment. This was a time he would and should always remember. His human had claimed him. She was crying and smiling, lips trembling as if the emotions she endured were too much to hold in anymore.

He kissed her, cleaned her lips with his, and held her gently as she deserved. She sobbed softly against him, cutting his heart in tiny slashes until she looked up at him and whispered, "Now you're mine for always."

And he was. From this moment on, he was all in. Whatever she needed to be happy, he would move mountains to give it to her. He breathed for her smile and would always do his best to earn it.

For always.

Kate was now his to protect.

Inside, his wolf howled because they were now bound in ways he hadn't been able to imagine.

Claimed as family, pack, lover, best friend, mate, sanctuary...home. Now, his Kate was everything.

SEVENTEEN

A soft rattle woke Dalton up from a deep sleep. He angled his ear toward the sound, confused as he struggled to escape the final folds of a dream he couldn't quite remember. Kate was sound asleep against his chest, and he tightened his arms around her fractionally.

The vibration sounded again.

His cell phone glowed from the small bedside table. With a grunt, he loosened himself from under Kate's cheek, settled her gently on the pillow, and scrubbed his hand down his face as he reached for the phone. It was a miracle the danged thing was getting reception. They were on the outskirts of Galena, and some places in the cabin got zero bars. With a glare at the time—*1:10 a.m.*—he accepted the call on a blocked number.

"What?" he answered quietly with a glance over his shoulder for his sleeping mate.

"I'm calling in my favor."

Dalton's face went slack. "Clayton?" He stood to go outside, eye on the reception on his phone, but the second he stood, the bars dipped down to one. Shit. "What kind of favor?"

"I have a kill order."

"What? Have you lost your damned mind? I'm not an enforcer. If you want to put down a problem shifter, give the order to one of your sons."

"This mission is off the books. I trust you'll be discreet, both to my sons and to your alpha."

"Link? Let me get this straight, in exchange for getting rid of the video, which would label you a decent person by the way, you want me to satisfy a kill order?"

"If you want that little sex tape to reappear to haunt your new mate again, tell me 'no.'" Clayton sounded off. Weird. Nervous, like he was bluffing. Like he *needed* Dalton to do this for him. He was scared.

"Who?"

Three heartbeats of silence preceded Clayton's answer. "Emanuel Vega."

"Vega?" Dalton gritted out. "He isn't a shifter, Clayton. He's human. You want me to run a kill order on a human?

I'm not a fucking man-eater. If you want a human murdered, send in a McCall."

"I need this done quietly—"

"Clayton—"

"I need it done quickly—"

"Clayton!"

"You'll do this," Clayton yelled into the phone, "or I'll do much more than re-upload your mate's video. You owe me. This is your duty now."

"Tell me why. I deserve that much. Tell me why you need Vega gone. Tell me why I have to do it alone."

"Don't pretend you're a real pack, Dalton."

"Fuck you, Clayton. You know nothing about our pack. Tell me why."

"Because he is a threat to you and your mate and all of us. You want to keep Kate safe? Cut Vega down at the legs, or there will be blood spilled. Shifter. Blood. I can't say more than that. I don't like giving a kill order on a human—"

"Don't like it, but you're still doing it. This is a declaration of war against the humans. You get that, right? And you've chosen me to be your assassin."

"He knows what you are."

"And he's done nothing with that information! Nothing. Until he does, I can't justify killing a human. I can't. You'll turn my wolf mad, and Link needs us steady under him. If I go down, the pack goes with me."

"I'm doing this for Link!" Clayton barked out. "He can't know, can't be involved. Your alpha is one year into the McCall Reset. Vera keeps me apprised. He still struggles to maintain control. He can't be in on this kill order or the bloodlust will push him over the edge. There is a reason the bears handle this shit, Dalton. They're built for blood, but you werewolves are different. You're weaker."

Dalton allowed a single, surprised laugh. Clayton really didn't know anything at all about werewolves or bears. Maybe Clayton was better with blood, but his sons, Ian, Jenner, and Tobias struggled a great deal with the kill orders they'd had to fulfill through the years. Killing always came at a cost. "Then do it yourself if your bear gives you such mental protection from taking an innocent human life—"

"Your first mistake is in thinking Vega is innocent." Clayton's voice went empty and strange. "You forget who you're talking to. I alone hold the power to destroy you and everyone you love. Do it tonight, do it quietly, call me when it's finished, and we'll be even. Just you. Fuck this up, and you'll never find a hole deep enough to hide your mate from my wrath."

216

The phone clicked, and the glow of the screen faded to black.

Fury filled Dalton like red fog, bathing everything he saw in it. The moonlight drenched wooden walls, and the rafters above him turned crimson. He ran his hands through his hair and glared upward, searching for a way out of this. He'd only just gotten his happiness back, and this put everything in jeopardy. He'd known better than to trade favors with Clayton, even if it was to save Kate from that damned video. He'd made a deal with the devil, and now he would pay with his soul. Killing a human? Fuck. He'd be no better than the McCalls that Link and the Silvers had hunted down and ended last year. Killing humans was against shifter law. If he did this, it would give Clayton cause to put a kill order out on Dalton the minute he stepped out of line. It wasn't just him who was affected by this threat. He had Kate now, and her safety was being threatened to control him.

Kate's hand rested on his back, and he jolted still under her touch.

"You can't."

He slid her a look over his shoulder, and her emerald eyes were filled with such worry.

He swallowed hard. "How much did you hear?"

"Everything, both your side and his. Dalton, you can't," she repeated.

"I know. But you don't know the man on the other end of that line. He's king."

"King murderer, and you'll be his mercenary. That's no king, Dalton. Vega is an asshole and knows more than he should, but he's just a man fighting some inner demons we don't understand. He hasn't done anything to the pack and hasn't said a word to me since he was fired."

"Should I wait until he does?" Dalton asked, standing to his full height. He paced the length of the bed. "Clayton sounded scared of him. Scared of *Vega*, Kate. A human. Clayton isn't afraid of anyone."

"Dalton, you've told me about Clayton, about the type of father he was, how he hid who he was from his sons for years while he gave them kill orders to enforce. What about the secrets he kept about Link's father and his interest in the McCall curse? He had Vera Turned against her will and trapped on an island of psychopaths for *years*, Dalton. He has moments of good. *Moments*. But the in-between times, you can't be certain what angle he is playing."

"What are you suggesting I do, Kate? He can ruin us. He can hurt you. His hands are in everything in my world."

"Our world now, and I won't let you sacrifice your wolf so he can cover your hands in blood."

"What do you think I should do?"

"I think you should slow down and think about this. One thing I learned with raising sled dogs was the importance of numbers. One winter, we had a wolf problem. Just one, so we thought. A female. Night after night, she came closer and closer to the shelters, howling louder and louder. Calling to our dogs. Tempting them."

"A lure?"

"Yes. And when one of our lead dogs broke his chain one night to follow her, he was killed by her pack, and all we found were bones picked clean in the woods. Why would Clayton require you to do this alone? Why would he separate you from the pack?"

Chills blasted up his arms, and he stopped his pacing. She was right. He was in it, already planning on ways to kill Vega discreetly to protect what he'd found with Kate. He was ready to run off into the woods on Clayton's whim with no real explanation of why Vega needed to die at his teeth, and his teeth alone.

Dread pumped through him with every beat of his pounding heart.

Clayton was the lure.

EIGHTEEN

Dalton sat on the front porch, his shoulder muscles bunched and tensed, making the phoenix on his back look fierce.

The soft, constant snarl was the only sound in the quiet night. It wasn't the happy or satisfied sound he rattled off when they were intimate. This was different. It was chill inducing. It was a hard warning that someone was going to bleed tonight.

"You smell like terror," he said in a voice too low and too gravelly to be mistaken for human. And when he ghosted her a glance over his shoulder, his eyes were so light they were almost yellow, glowing from the inside out like twin flames.

If she hadn't been scared before, Dalton would've pushed her over the edge.

Mustering her courage, she padded over the porch and rested her palm lightly on his shoulder. "It's time," she said.

Dalton arched his eerie gaze to the woods. "Do you remember the plan?"

"Yes," she whispered.

He narrowed his eyes at her, and she gulped down the coward in her middle. "Yes," she said louder, more firmly.

"I'm going to Vega's land. I'll do as Clayton says, but I want you safe. I want you to stay here, stay inside, don't come out, no matter what, and keep a rifle right beside you. Anyone who walks through that door that you don't recognize, you blow them to hell, do you understand?"

"Yes," she said, the answer more confident than she actually felt.

He was going out there after Vega. A hundred things could go wrong. "Dalton—"

"Don't. I won't be able to do this if you put your worry on me. Tonight I'll become a man-eater, and I need you steady beside me. I need you to anchor me."

Her stomach dipped to the floor with what he planned to do, but she blinked hard and nodded, determined to stay strong for him. Her mate stood in a blur. One moment he was sitting below her on the porch, and the next instant he had her pulled flush against him, his hand cupping her

222

cheek, his lips harsh on hers. He moved his kisses down her jaw and to her neck, gripped her hair. Too tight. "Listen to me," he whispered so softly between kisses she could barely hear him. "I can smell them in the woods. Vega isn't alone. Remember the plan. Let me draw them away."

She wanted to beg him to stay. Wanted to plead with him not to leave her alone to go willingly into this trap, but he'd already made up his mind, and now he smelled of fur and nothing else. Clinging to him, she closed her eyes and absorbed the last moment she was guaranteed with the man she loved.

He kissed her once more, too hard, too rough, then turned and jogged lithely down the stairs and into the yard. With one last yellow glance, Dalton's head snapped backward and his body bowed as he grunted in pain. He fell to his hands and knees as the sound of breaking bones echoed through the clearing. His teeth were gritted against the pain as his face slowly elongated, stretching his skin until he ripped and reshaped.

Kate wanted to look away. She wanted to run inside and bury her face in her pillow until Dalton's Change was over, but he was allowing her to see all of him, and the least she could do was stand her ground and be brave for him.

Minutes felt like hours as Dalton slowly disappeared and a massive black-furred wolf was conjured in his place. As he stood and shook his fur out, Kate's breath caught at how beautiful he was. How powerful and terrifying. He faced her, thick chest out, massive head high, ears erect, and his eyes burned like two suns against all that pitch black fur. He looked nothing like Miller's small, rangy-looking gray wolf. Dalton was a titan wolf with giant paws, and his eyes didn't have the look of madness in them. Dalton's hard expression said *be ready*. He bore his teeth once, white and jagged like scalpel tips, before he turned and trotted slowly into the woods, disappearing like a phantom into the night.

And now he would be hunted while she sat here huddled in the cabin, wondering what was happening out there in those woods, and hoping to hell everything was going according to plan. She cursed Clayton for whatever treachery he was pulling and backed slowly into the house. She felt watched out here, exposed, and the chills that had risen on her arms with the terrifying sound in Dalton's throat hadn't gone away when he'd left.

These woods were haunted right now.

She winced as her back hit the door frame. Her new bite mark still stung under the bandages Dalton had doctored her with. A stiff breeze washed through the trees, swaying branches and filling the woods with the soft creaking of the sturdy pines.

She turned to escape the lonely sound.

"Hello, traitor," Vega said from his seat on the couch.

She startled violently and gasped. He looked different. His shaved head, pallid skin, and bloodshot eyes were the same, but he wore a dark cloak with a hood that covered most of him, and he seemed calmer than she'd seen him in months. His eyes weren't shifting back and forth suspiciously anymore, but steady and black as onyx on her. A cruel smile lifted the corners of his lips, transforming his face into something ghastly.

"Wh-what are you doing in my house?"

"You mean your den?" Vega asked, forehead wrinkling deeply with the question. "You left your back door unlocked. Fatal move."

"Get out. We haven't done anything to you. Get out now!" she screamed.

"I saw you," he said, standing. He approached slowly, backing her toward the open door.

She slid a glance at the rifle hanging from pegs on the wall, but Vega angled himself between it and her with a wicked grin. "No guns, love. That's not how this works."

The loud shot of a rifle sounded outside, and she jumped. It was close, and the sound of a bullet connecting with something made a sickening *thunk* at the end.

"What I meant to say was guns won't work for you," Vega said, looking unsurprised. "Going on a wolf hunt, a wolf hunt, a wolf hunt," he sang in the soft, off-key notes of a madman.

"Dalton!" Kate screamed, bolting out the open door. She skidded across the porch and jumped over the stairs, landing hard in the yard, losing and catching her balance in a moment before she sprinted toward the woods. No, no, no!

"Bring her to me," Vega ordered in a bored voice.

She was almost to the tree line. If she could just make it out of the glow of the porch light, she could get lost in the trees. But something was behind her. Something big and too fast. Her boots squished through the mud, and it bogged her down, but whoever chased her suffered from no such problem. She could feel him breathing on her neck as she pushed her legs harder. She could sense him behind her. Evil. These men were evil. Adrenaline dumped into her veins as she ran for her life—for Dalton's life. She had to help him. Had to save him because everything had gone wrong. This wasn't part of the plan! Vega was hunting Dalton, not her. Everything was falling apart.

Kate screamed as something hit her like a cannonball from behind. She hit the mud hard, but harsh hands flipped her over and picked her up, then slammed her back down. Glowing eyes, crooked teeth, a hungry smile, and then his scarred knuckles were barreling toward her face too fast for her to do more than lurch to the side and take the hit across her cheek. She gasped in pain as her vision doubled. Half of her face felt ripped off, but her attacker wasn't done as she struggled for the knife Dalton had made her put in the back of her jeans. The man was sitting on top of her, straddling her, weighing her down. She fought like an injured wild animal, but he picked her up by the throat and lifted her feet off the ground. Clawing and scrabbling at his hands, she kicked at him and writhed, trying desperately to loose herself.

"Harlan!" Vega yelled. "Let her down."

The grip disappeared in a moment, and she fell to her knees, choking and sucking at the few air particles that could make it past her tightened throat.

Warmth trickled down her cheek, and her face throbbed in rhythm to her heartbeat, but she couldn't pass out. Not now. Not when there was still work to do. Gritting her teeth against the pain, she sucked in as big a breath as her throat would allow and pulled Dalton's long hunting knife from the sheath at her back. Harlan was turning away from her now to face Vega.

"You said we would kill them," Harlan whined.

"And we will, but not like that. There are traditions to uphold, dear Harlan. Bring her inside."

In a rush, she mentally rattled off the arteries in the human body and determined the one she could reach, the one that would do the most damage. With a grunt, she pressed the knife against his leg as Harlan turned and with all her strength, she bore down and split him open.

"Fuck!" he screamed, holding his thigh. Red seeped between his fingertips in waves. "You stupid bitch." Harlan fell onto her as she jammed the knife upward, but he was too fast this time and wrenched the knife from her hand with a painful jerk of her wrist.

"Harlan!" Vega ordered. "I said bring her into the cabin. It's almost time."

Rage filled Harlan's too bright eyes, but his face morphed into a smile. "I can't wait to watch you burn," he whispered, inches away from her face.

Burn? She yelped in pain as he pulled her up by the hair and shoved her toward the cabin.

"That was a surprise with the knife," he gritted out from behind her as he shoved her roughly again. "I like being surprised. Vera used to surprise me. It turned me on, but Vega won't let us touch you like that."

She should definitely keep him talking and stall. "You know Vera?"

"We all do," he said darkly.

Kate skidded to a stop in horror as three other men melted out of the woods, all shrouded in the same dark hoods Vega and Harlan wore.

"Everyone thought poor Vera was trapped on Perl with misfits for her to experiment on. We weren't misfits. We were bodyguards, making sure she kept on task, making sure her medicines worked, making sure she could suppress our animals." He laughed, but it sounded off. Insane. "Dalton isn't dead." Harlan gripped her shirt and pushed her forward so hard she stumbled to her knees. "Not yet."

"Where is he?" she gasped out.

"You'll be happy to know that his wolf won't feel a thing when he hangs from that noose. Clayton gave us some of Vera's medicine to cure him. Safety precautions, you see. Werewolves are...unpredictable."

"Dalton!" she called as desperation clawed its way up her throat.

Vega pulled her up by the scruff of her shirt and dragged her struggling body to the porch stairs, then turned her.

"No," she said in horror as she dragged her gaze to the chopping block one of the cloaked men had propped under Dalton's bare feet. He was naked, skin smeared with dirt, and red streamed down his shoulder, covering half of his entire torso. He was human again, hands bound behind his back, and around his neck was an old-fashioned hangman's noose.

"Let her go," Dalton said low, eyes over her shoulder on Vega.

"I saw you," Vega gritted out. "I saw you bite her tonight from that window." Beside her, Vega's finger jammed at the picture window over their bed. "I sat in these woods hoping Kate could still be saved, but you sank your teeth into her back and ruined any chance she had of surviving me. Filthy, fucking, dirty *whore*!" he yelled so loud against her hear, her head rang and spun. "You fucking werewolves couldn't stay quiet, could you? Do you want a history lesson, Kate?" He gripped the back of her neck so tightly she hunched at the excruciating pain. "In the old days, we annihilated evil in a civilized manner. We were revered. Feared. Held on a pedestal by the humans who were afraid that you would come in the night and make off with their children. Dawson." He spat the name like a curse. "Do you know what your ancestors did to us, Dalton? All they had to do was die. Hang and burn. Instead, they annihilated our last remaining faction. Jeremiah Dawson. Luke Dawson. Those are names in our history books because they ended what we had held sacred for centuries. But you couldn't stay quiet, could you? You couldn't stop fucking up, hurting people, killing innocents. I don't blame you. That's just what monsters do."

"The McCalls drew the attention," Dalton said, struggling against the two cloaked men who held him in place. "We haven't done anything."

Vega laughed harshly. "Are you serious? You haven't done anything? You've evolved, Dalton. You don't poison people with your bite anymore. You can blend in better and make it harder for us to hunt you. And now Clayton's little pet fox shifter made a fucking cure not only for the McCall line, but for female offspring. Fina Clotila McCall will be your queen. That infant will grow up to rally you all, and she's only the first. Do you really think we can let that happen? Do you think we can allow you to keep twice the amount of offspring you bore before? Do you think we can let you keep female breeders that will strengthen your line, make you more numerous, make you braver? No!"

A sickening look of realization had taken Dalton's face as Vega had talked. "Kate, look at me," Dalton said, chest heaving as he struggled violently against his restraints. "I didn't know what he was. Don't go in the house. Don't let them take you in the house, Kate. Do you hear me?" he yelled as Vega dragged her backward. "Run!"

Harlan was limping badly but was pouring something onto the house. Her throat clogged with fear as she smelled it. Gasoline. They were going to burn her alive, and they were making Dalton watch.

"Vega, you missed the war. You missed it," Dalton pleaded. "We killed the McCalls who drew attention. There's a cure for the rest of us!"

"The only cure for the devil inside of you is death," Vega said, dragging Kate inside, inch by inch.

"Why are you doing this?" she screamed, clinging onto the doorframe.

Vega yanked her in and slammed her onto the ground right beside the couch. "Because." He glared down at her with the fire of hatred in his dark eyes. "I'm a Hell Hunter."

The long note of a lone wolf sounded outside, lifting with the breeze. Vega froze and shot a shocked look at the window. Shaking his head slowly back and forth, he murmured, "No. Clayton told Dalton to hunt me alone. He *told* him."

"My wolves don't answer to Clayton," Link said, boots echoing hollowly over the fox tunnel and root cellar he'd come through. His eyes burned bright white, and his face was the terrifying mask of a death bringer. "They answer to me."

The roar of a bear out in the woods rattled the house, and another answered from farther away.

"We knew Clayton answered to someone," Link snarled, "and now we know who. The last of the Hell Hunters. Pity he isn't here to watch you Turn."

"Y-you can't Turn me," Vega whispered. "You can't."

"Mmm," Link said with a noncommittal shrug. "Not a werewolf, perhaps. But I have this friend who is a bitey little thing. It'll be full circle, Vega. You were part of the machine that had her Turned against her will."

Outside, men were screaming, but through the noise, a soft snarl rattled from the open doorway. Vera's fox stood there, legs splayed, teeth bared. Scrambling from the floor, Kate bolted for the rifle on the wall and aimed it at Vega who was trapped between Link's murderous eyes and Vera's snapping teeth.

"Vera's a clever little fox," Link said. "When Clayton asked for vials of the cure, she did, in fact, give him a cure. Just the wrong one."

All hell had broken loose outside with snarling, the scream of a panther, and the roaring of the bears, but just above the chaotic noise, a throatier snarl sounded from the doorway behind Vera. Kate's shoulders sagged with relief as Dalton's black wolf stepped inside of the house. He was alive.

Link canted his head. "You see, Vera figured out a cure for our painfully slow shifts. You didn't stifle Dalton's wolf when you injected him, Vega." Link smiled slowly, baring his teeth, and his cheek twitched with barely concealed fury. "You made it easier for him to Change."

Vera scrabbled toward Vega, nails cutting into the wood floors, and in a flash, she was on the other side, standing near Link, her gold eyes narrowed on Vega as he lifted his hand in shock. Trickles of blood seeped from a puncture wound at the base of his thumb.

"Does it burn?" Link asked. "Vera said it burned like fire in her veins when she was bitten. That's the poison. That's your animal growing inside of you. And now you'll die a *monster*, just like the ones you hunt."

"No," he said, eyes wide on his hand. "This isn't happening. I was careful. Clayton obeys my orders. Only mine!" he yelled in a booming voice as he clutched his bleeding hand to his middle.

He rushed toward Kate, but she pumped the shotgun in her hands and rested her finger on the trigger with a warning shake of her head. Vega skidded to a stop, dark eyes wide with realization. He's lost. There was nowhere to run, nowhere to hide, and outside, his men had gone silent.

Link clicked his tongue behind his teeth. "Making shifters watch you burn their innocent families before you hang them? Centuries of wrong-doing, and you tote what you are like a badge of honor." The alpha twitched his head, his snow-colored eyes hard on Vega. "Dalton, your mate smells like blood, and your den reeks of gasoline. Vengeance is yours to take. Let the Dawson line end the Hell Hunters once again."

In an instant, Vega fell forward and was dragged clawing and scrabbling against the cabin floor until he was outside.

And then all was quiet.

NINETEEN

"They were going to hang him," Kate whispered, sagging to her knees. The shotgun was too heavy to keep aimed anymore, so she lowered it. "Link, they were going to hang Dalton and burn me alive."

"No, we wouldn't have let them." Link knelt in front of her and lifted her chin, then winced at her face. "Kate, you're hurt."

"I know him. Vega. Or...I knew him," she corrected with a frown. "He worked with me for years, and he was going to kill me. Torture me."

Link swallowed hard and shot a worried glance at the door. "Kate," he whispered, "before Dalton comes back in here, you have to be okay."

Was she even touching the ground anymore? Or was she floating. She must be in shock. "Because Dalton's a man-eater now."

"Vega wasn't a man," Vera said in a shaky voice from her hands and knees behind Link. She stumbled to her feet and wiped red off her mouth. "He died a shifter, and none of those men outside were human either. Dalton will have one less technicality to deal with."

"They knew you," Kate murmured, a tear fleeing her eye and streaming down her cheek. "Those men were on Perl Island with you. They were shifters hunting shifters, Vera. Shifters hunting shifters," she repeated.

Link plucked the gun gently from her grasp and unloaded it, then set it back on the pegs where it belonged. Vera pulled Kate up into a tight embrace.

Outside, the murmur of men's voices carried through the open door.

"You did good," Vera said, squeezing her tighter. "Do you hear me? We saw you fighting, saw you stalling while Link was headed into the house through that tunnel. Brave little human. You bought us all time to get into position so that none of us would get hurt."

Kate's face crumpled with a sob as she hugged Vera tightly. "Everyone's okay?"

"Yeah. Well, Tobias probably has a face full of wereporcupine quills because of Harlan the beef-jerky-smelling traitor, and Chance and the Silvers might be clawed up a little. But Elyse, Lena, and Nicole are holed up with the babies, safe and sound. We're all okay because you called in the pack. It was smart of you and Dalton to be suspicious of Clayton. I've watched him play too many sides to ever really trust him. And oooh, his boys are going to bleed him for this one."

"What about Dalton. Will he be okay?"

"He was shot, but it looked like it went clean through his shoulder. His shifter healing will fix it in a few days."

"That's not what I meant," Kate whispered. "Will his wolf be okay?"

Vera eased her back to arm's length and leveled her with a stony, serious look. "He's a Dawson, not a McCall. He'll be fine. But maybe let's get you cleaned up to make it easier on him, okay?"

"My face has a pulse," Kate muttered, touching her cheek gently as Vera pulled her by the hand toward the bathroom. "And by the way, I'm getting black-out curtains for that window behind our bed because Vega definitely said he watched Dalton bite me, which means he saw a whole lot of other mortifying stuff." Chills rippled against her skin in waves. She felt so violated by everything that had happened.

The soft *shush-shush* sound of water hitting the house sounded.

When Kate froze to listen, Vera explained, "Sounds like the boys are washing off the gasoline."

Those awful Hell Hunters had tried to burn the house. Tried to burn her *home* while Dalton was supposed to watch her blaze into ashes right along with it. Another wave of anger rippled across her skin, flushing her with heat as she gripped the edges of the bathroom sink. There was a small, seeping cut on her cheek that wouldn't need more than butterfly bandages and some discoloring that said she was going to have one epic black eye over the next couple of days, but other than that, she just looked pale and muddy and pissed. The shock was wearing off now, leaving more and more room for fury.

She scooped water from the trickling faucet and scrubbed her face clean of Harlan's mistreatment, and when the last of the mud from her face and arms had trickled down the drain, she changed her clothes and pulled her damp hair into a messy bun. Gathering her courage, she lifted her chin primly and sauntered out to the living room where Tobias sat at the table while Vera plucked enormous porcupine quills from his shoulder with needle-nose pliers. Kate would've offered her nursing skills, but when she opened her mouth to do so, Vera rested her forehead against Tobias's temple and whispered something low as she laid her hand gently on his bare chest. He closed his too-bright eyes and sighed. Such a tender moment shouldn't be interrupted, and Vera looked like she knew what she was doing.

Link paced the kitchen, talking on the phone. The air in here felt heavy and suffocating. "If you ever even talk to one of my wolves again, Clayton, I'll rip your fucking head off your shoulders." He ended the call and threw the phone against the wall. Plastic pieces shattered, skittering across the floorboards. Eyes blazing, he growled out, "Vega has been feeding money, intel, and the kill orders to the king asshole himself. Clayton has been answering to a damned Hell Hunter this entire time. He said Vega promised not to go after his sons, or me, if Clayton did his bidding. Vega gave the kill order on Dalton after he saw Dalton bite Kate. He went nuts and threatened to hunt us all if Clayton didn't give them Dalton."

Vera plucked another quill from Tobias's arm and pressed a rag onto his skin to staunch the bleeding. "I knew Clayton was playing too many sides of something. I could feel it but I couldn't figure out who he was dealing with. When he asked for the cure a few days ago, I smelled a rat. I just got this sick feeling he was going to take some poor sucker's animal away. He was going to render someone helpless, so I gave him a serum to speed up the Change instead. I thought it would give whoever he was hunting a chance to defend themselves, you know? Make it a fair fight and all. I can't believe it was for Dalton." She shook her head and looked disgusted. "How could Clayton answer to those assholes? How could he try to sacrifice one of your wolves to protect you? Link, it wouldn't protect you at all. Losing pack members could destroy your wolf, even after the McCall Reset."

Link shook his head and stared out the front window with a faraway look. "He said he was trying to keep the casualties to a minimum until he could figure out how to end the growing problem. Keep your enemies closer and all that."

"I don't give a shit what his excuses are," Tobias said in an empty voice. "He's done. Ian and Jenner will back me. He's cut off from our family. He pulls us in and shares fractions of the truth, then does something despicable again. His moral compass is broken. That was his last chance to be a decent person." He dragged his gaze to Kate. "I'm sorry for what's happened, and I'm sorry for my father's part in it."

"It's not your fault," she said.

Ian and Jenner were nowhere to be seen, but Chance sat in a chair against the wall, watching his alpha. He wore jeans, but a long claw mark and several puncture wounds were seeping red across his ribs.

When Chance inhaled harshly and looked up at her, his eyes were such a light, icy green, it almost hurt to look at them. Without a word, he stood and hugged her tightly, then clapped her on the back too roughly. He cleared his throat and hooked his hands on his hips, gaze on the floor. "If anything would've happened to you…" Chance glanced at the open doorway, then back at her, looking tortured. "I know what April First cost Dalton. I was there for all of it, and I was scared he… I'm just really glad you're okay."

Kate squeezed his shoulder and rested her cheek on it for a moment. "I'm okay, are you?"

"I'll mend. Don't worry about me."

"Where is he?"

Chance twitched his head. "Outside." As she strode for the door, he asked, "Kate?"

She pressed her palm against the frame and turned. "Yeah?"

"I'm glad Dalton chose you." Chance's voice cracked on the last word.

Heart too big for her chest, she nodded. "Me, too."

Offering him a half smile, she made her way out onto the porch. She expected carnage, but the ground was clear and the bodies were gone. That was probably where Ian and Jenner were. Their time as enforcers would've taught them how to dispose of bodies, especially after kill orders. There was a long smear of red along the porch boards where Vega had been dragged. Kate swallowed hard and stepped over the streak carefully.

Just outside of the porch light, Dalton worked to cut his hanging noose down from the ancient spruce tree on the edge of the yard. He wore low-slung jeans, but his back was bare, and the phoenix tattoo was stark against his pale skin. Vera had been right. The shot looked like it had gone straight through his shoulder, and though red painted his back like a canvas, he wasn't favoring it as he sawed at the thick rope with the knife Harlan had wrenched from her hand.

"You shouldn't be cutting your own rope," Kate said, her throat closing around the words as she ran her hand up his back just beside his spine.

One last cut, and Dalton yanked the rope out of the branches above. He didn't turn around, didn't look at her.

Her voice pitched low, she murmured, "I thought they were going to hang you."

Dalton turned slowly under her touch, his eyes hard as he lifted his chin to expose his neck. "They did."

Kate gripped her middle and barely avoided doubling over at the sight of the deeply etched, bloody rope burn around his throat. "Oh, Dalton."

He blinked rapidly, his gaze full of so many things. Despair. Worry. Pain. "It'll scar, and you'll always look at it and remember tonight. I can cut down the hanging tree, but I can't undo the hanging scar."

She took the last step toward him, closing the space between them, needing to feel his warm skin against her to convince herself he was still here and not some ghost or figment of her imagination. Dalton angled his shoulder away, though, and countered her step-for-step, warning in his gaze.

Hurt by his intentional distance, she stopped her advance. "H-how did you get away?"

"Apparently Vega didn't study how Hell Hunters did hangings in the old days. They dropped me from two low, and the rope is new. It had too much stretch to break my neck. I nearly suffocated instead before my wolf pushed out of me and slipped the noose. I thought whoever shot me had injected me with the cure to put my animal to sleep, but my wolf was there, right under the surface, ready for me to reach him. The Change was instant, and the rope didn't hold me. And before that, Chance's wolf was under me, trying to prop me up, exposing his back to a fucking panther to try to keep me breathing. They were *shifters*, Kate." Dalton stabbed his knife deep into the tree trunk, then bent down, plucked the rope from the mud and began looping coils from his palm to elbow to his palm again. "I always thought it would be humans to come after us, but it was our own damned people." Dalton lifted his golden gaze to her throbbing cheek, then down to the forest floor. In a tortured voice, he murmured, "You wouldn't have been hurt if I'd been strong enough to stay away from you."

"And I would've been hurt worse if you did. This," she said, gesturing to her cheek, "is nothing compared to the pain I was in before I met you. The loneliness, the fear. Nightmares, sleeplessness, restlessness, helplessness, never feeling like enough. You changed *all* of that."

"And now how will you feel, Kate?" he asked. "How can you feel safe now? I pledged my body to protect you, and you got hurt. You were attacked. Our home was doused in gasoline with you in it. You were hit by a man, and I was hung. How will you ever look at my face, at the scar on my neck, and feel safe again?"

"Because I'm stronger now, Dalton! I'm different. I'm changed because of you. Because I have something to fight for now. You won't cut down the hanging tree. You'll carve

245

our initials in it, and we'll take it back. And that scar on your neck will be so beautiful to me. You know why? Because the last moments I saw you with that awful rope around your neck, your eyes were on me, and you were telling me to run. You were about to hang, and you were trying to save me. You did save me. You balked against Clayton's order and called in your pack. You ended Vega, you kept fighting to live, and now I don't have to…" Her shoulders sagged as a sob clawed its way up her throat. "I don't have to bury you and try to survive what your loss would do to me. Please don't push me away."

Dalton dropped the loops of rope and pulled her into an embrace so tight she couldn't breathe, but she didn't care. He was warm and alive against her, and they would be all right.

"I'm sorry, I'm sorry," he chanted between kisses laid on top of her hair.

His body was shaking, so she clung tighter to him and pressed her cheek against his chest just to feel and hear his steady heartbeat. That sound was everything right now.

"I thought I was going to lose you," he rasped. "I thought I was going to lose everything again, and I couldn't stop it. I had to trust Link and Chance and the Silvers instead of being able to protect you all by myself, and it kills me."

"Baby," she whispered, easing back. "That's the way it's supposed to be with our pack."

"Our pack," he repeated, brushing the pad of his thumb lightly under the cut on her cheek.

"Yeah. It's not you or me against the world anymore, Dalton." She smiled slowly. "We've got them, and they have us."

Her words weren't just a balm because her mate was worried for her. She had Dalton now, and he'd given her more than he understood. He'd given her a family. He'd given her the protection of his body, but also of his pack and the Silvers, who had taken a huge risk tonight just to make sure she was okay. She didn't know what the coming years would bring or if the danger from the Hell Hunters was truly over, but she knew one thing.

She wouldn't face them alone.

Dalton was unwavering in his devotion for her. He was trustworthy.

He had given her a pack, a home, and unconditional love. He'd given her the promise of forever with the ring that clung to her finger and the fresh claiming mark on her back. He made her that same promise every time he told her he loved her, every time he kissed her. But more than that, he'd given her a future unburdened of fear.

Standing on her tiptoes, Kate kissed his lips gently and reveled in the sound of the content growl that softly rattled his throat.

Her Dalton, her wolf. Her mate.

The Hell Hunters hadn't broken them as they'd intended.

They'd strengthened them instead.

EPILOGUE

"He's here. Shut your mouth holes!" Vera sang in an opera voice as she ran through the Silver Summit Outfitters lodge, her glittery high heels clacking across the hardwood floors.

A new wave of nerves took Kate. She wrung her hands and took a deep, steadying breath. Dalton was finally back after a weeklong guided tour with Chance and a group of fishermen.

Link hugged her to his side and whispered, "Are you ready?"

"No. Yes! I was so scared the timing wouldn't work out."

Link's face split into a smile, his gray eyes dancing as he said, "April first, and he's back right on time, just like Lennard said he would be."

It was a good sign that Dalton hadn't wanted to binge drink and disappear this year. Chance had said this was the first year Dalton had wanted to keep everything normal, and then he'd thanked Kate for starting that change in his cousin. Silly Chance. Couldn't he see? Dalton was the one who'd saved her.

The butterflies in her stomach were flapping double-time as she grinned at the small crowd of their closest friends. She pressed her finger to her lips. "Shhh. Give me five minutes, and I'll bring him in."

Vera, Elyse, and Lena were all grins as she shot them a wink and headed for the door. Nicole handed her the new puppy Kate had bought, a little red and white troublemaker named Sasha Two. With an emotional smile, Nicole hugged Kate's shoulders tightly. Words weren't needed now. Nicole understood how big this was.

Cuddling the fluffy little husky pup close, Kate let herself quietly out of the heavy front door.

Over the past year, this lodge had become a home away from home, as it was for Dalton. She visited often when he was out on tours, usually hitching a bush plane ride with Lena when she came up to visit her mate, Jenner. Kate had grown close to the Silvers over the months, but Nicole had become like a sister to her, and Fina like a niece. Good packs were like that, she supposed.

The beauty of this place awed her every time she looked over the clearing to the sprawling deck down by the water's edge, the river beyond, and the snow-peaked mountains beyond that. Kodiak was unsettled and untamed. Wild, just like her mate.

She was stunned to stillness when she saw him riding through the trees on a buckskin horse. The hanging scar was half-hidden under his dark scruff, and his eyes were black as pitch under the bill of his worn baseball cap. A backpack clung to his wide shoulders, and his torso moved in time with the smooth gait of his horse. He was talking to a client on the horse next to him and hadn't seen her yet. Usually, he spotted her right away, but he didn't expect her this trip, so she took the moment to enjoy watching him work. Oh, Dalton was a capable man, as he'd shown her over the past year. He was a good provider, a patient teacher, and an incredibly skilled tracker. There was nothing he couldn't do, and watching him dismount his horse with a smooth swing of his leg, she was taken again with how lucky she'd been to find him. He took so much responsibility on his shoulders and never once had she seen him buckle or heard him complain. He was just that strong and resilient. And hers.

Chance rushed to unload the clients' belongings as Dalton led the horses into the corral and pulled their saddles off one-by-one, resting each on the wooden fence to pull into the barn when they were through. Chance knew about the surprise, though, and from here, she could hear him rushing her mate to hurry up.

With a giggle, she toted a wiggling Sasha Two down the porch stairs. Dalton caught her movement and jerked his attention to her. A breathtaking smile slid slowly over his face as he began to walk toward her, and then jog.

He met her in the middle and caught her up in a hug. "Damn, wife, you're a sight for sore eyes. What are you doing here? I was coming straight home tonight." With a sudden frown, he eased back and studied her face. "What's wrong?"

She laughed and rubbed her cheek against the thick scruff on his jaw. He always looked like a sexy mountain man when he finished a guided tour. "I couldn't wait any longer to show you our first dog. It's happening, Dalton. Tobias flew her in two days ago from her breeder near Anchorage. She has champion bloodlines, her grandfather led a team to second place in the Iditarod last year, and she's all ours. She's the start of it all, Dalton. Link even made us this gorgeous wooden sign to go over the driveway. It says

Dawson Huskies. We figured you'd be the one to want to hang it."

The worry melted from Dalton's dark eyes, and his smile came easy again. "What's her name?"

"Sasha Two."

"Perfect," he murmured, settling Kate on her feet. He took the ten-week-old pup from her arms and held her up, staring thoughtfully into her blue eyes. When the puppy yipped and wiggled her little curly tail, Kate almost lost the hold on her emotions. This wasn't done yet.

"She's not your only surprise," Kate said, tugging his hand toward the lodge.

"What?" Dalton asked, laughing nervously like he'd missed a joke somehow. He allowed her to lead him across the yard and up the porch before he balked at the door.

With one last look at the confusion that had commandeered his face, she pushed the door open.

The small crowd erupted into cheering, whooping, and whistling. From behind, Chance gripped Dalton's shoulder and shook him slowly before he sidled around him and joined the others. Vera and Nicole were already crying.

His smile turned to bafflement as he stepped into the sprawling entryway. He lifted his gaze to the giant hand-written *congratulations* sign that hung over the stairs. He cast an uncertain look to the dining table that was lined with food, homemade beer, moonshine, and the green, glittery, three tiered cake on the end—Vera's idea, of course.

"Are we getting married again?" he asked in confusion. "I thought you wanted the small wedding."

"No," Kate said through an excited grin. "Our wedding under the hanging tree was perfect."

"Oh." His dark eyebrows furrowed, and he looked at Sasha Two, who was currently chewing the undone top button of his sweater.

"It's not her either," Kate said as the cheering died down. She pulled his palm to her lips, pressed a kiss there, then leaned her cheek against it. "Five years ago, April First hurt you deeply."

Dalton swallowed hard and cast a quick look around, then back to her with a slight shake of his head. "I don't understand."

Her eyes burned with tears as she pulled his hand down to cup her belly, growing tighter everyday with their child. "Now we're taking April back."

Dalton's eyes filled, and he shook his head. "Don't tease me, wife," he whispered.

"I wouldn't. I've been waiting until April first to tell you. It's been so hard keeping it quiet from you."

"Everyone knows?" he asked, chest heaving as he scanned the faces of the people who meant the most to them.

Vera sniffled and nodded. "I've already been working, just in case it's a girl."

"Oh my God," Dalton said in a huff, sinking down to his knees. He settled Sasha Two on the floor and cupped the slight swell of Kate's belly with both hands. His shoulders shook as he pressed his lips against her stomach.

Warm tears streaked down Kate's cheeks as she closed her eyes and ran her fingers through his hair. "You're going to be a great daddy," she whispered.

He lifted his gaze to her, now bright and gold. Beautiful. She hoped their child had his wild eyes.

"I'm going to be a dad," he murmured. He pressed another kiss to her stomach and stared at it. "I'm going to be your dad."

Chance lowered to his knees beside Dalton and hugged his shoulders, gripping his shirt, and Link knelt behind Dalton, hand on his back as he swallowed over and over, his eyes lightened to the color of snow. One by one, the others approached and touched Dalton, and at last, Kate sank to her knees and hugged his neck.

Dalton cupped her belly, rubbing it in slow, gentle circles as he held her close. "You've given me everything," he whispered against her ear.

"No," she said, smiling at the people surrounding them who had played such a pivotal part in this moment. "We gave each other everything."

The End

Want More of These Characters?

Up Next in This Series

Chance Fur Hire
(Bears Fur Hire, Book 6)

Sneak Peek

Chapter One

Emily Vega was going to destroy the Galena pack.

Listening intently for any signs of life, she pushed open the door to the cabin. The *creeeak* of the wood sent shivers down her spine. Was she afraid? Hell, yes. Who wouldn't be if they knew what kind of monsters the Dawsons and their alpha really were. They were bloodthirsty murderers, and they'd taken everything from her.

Her vengeance would be felt through the entire shifter community after this. That was her pledge. It would be a warning to the others that she was coming. That they were being hunted.

With a steadying breath that blasted crystallized air in front of her face, she scanned the open cabin, from the exposed beams and the high pitch of the roof to the kitchen with its wooden counters and the living room with its dark leather couches. There was a towering stone fireplace that was barren and cold, and the wood burning stove in the corner was open with fresh tinder and firewood inside, ready to be lit when Dalton and his wife, Kate, returned from Silver Summit Outfitters.

As the breeze kicked up outside, the trees swayed and croaked behind her. Narrowing her eyes over her shoulder, she swatted at the hairs that had electrified on her neck. These damned woods were haunted by her father, and his soul wouldn't rest until she avenged him.

A fresh sense of urgency gripped her as she tiptoed through the house, placing the bugs where the Dawsons would never find them. One inside a decorative vase on an antique table in the corner, one under the lip of the countertop, and one in the drawer of the bedside table next to the bed.

It was a pity someone had put thick curtains over the large window behind the bed because her spying would be much easier with a clear view into the cabin at night. She would have to rely on her hearing to hunt the monsters that lived here.

One last bug under a porch floorboard, and she made her way to the shed out back. Uncle Victor said one of the Dawsons, Chance, lived out here when he visited. He would be an easy mark to gain access to the pack. Dumb animals, driven by the instinct to procreate. He was the last unmated wolf in the pack and would be the first to bleed for what they had done to her father.

His shed was more like a small log cabin with a wood burning stove much like the one inside the big house. A cot sat against the wall, the covers rumpled and unmade. Emily lifted the blanket and inhaled deeply. Huh. She'd expected the wild musk of wolf fur, but it smelled different. Good even. Like masculine body spray. With a frown, she dropped the soft fabric and took a step back.

She couldn't afford to see them as human. They weren't. They were monsters who had to be cut down. Her father had told her that from birth, and Uncle Victor had ensured she was trained to hunt them in case something like this ever happened.

A picture frame poked out from under the disturbed bedding, and carefully she plucked it from its hiding place. It was a photograph of a strapping blond-haired man with his arm slung over the shoulders of a man who looked quite his opposite. Dark hair, dark eyes, and an empty smile, as if he was sad. No, not sad. Monsters didn't feel emotions like that. He looked vacant because he was a demon.

Canting her head, she studied the blond-haired man. Chiseled jaw and bright green eyes with eyebrows so light in color, they were barely there. His bright-white smile looked genuine, as if he was mid-laugh. This was the crafty one. The wolf who could blend in and pretend to be human. Pretend to be normal.

A wave of hatred washed over her. She didn't know the exact details of the night her father had died, but she did know that one of these two men had killed him in cold blood.

Emily shoved the picture back where it had been and silently made her escape from the shed. She couldn't afford to get confused or unfocused, no matter what the werewolf looked or smelled like. He wasn't human. He wasn't.

She closed the door softly behind her and made sure to step on the grassy patches in the yard to avoid putting her footprints in the mud. With any luck, the Dawsons would come back in a few days, long after her scent had dissipated.

Gritting her teeth, Emily made her way to her dad's truck, climbed behind the wheel, and turned the engine. With one last look at the shed in the back, she stamped down the feeling of uncertainty that was snaking through her gut in an inky tendril. She hit the gas—the faster she escaped this place, the more certain she would feel in her task.

Dad had hunted these creatures for a reason, and Uncle Victor wanted retribution before he succumbed to the ever growing lull of his death bed.

She was the only one who could end this.

She was the only one who could make the Galena pack pay for what they'd stolen from her.

She, Emily Vega, was the last of the Hell Hunters.

Chance Fur Hire

(Bears Fur Hire, Book 6)

About the Author

T.S. Joyce is devoted to bringing hot shifter romances to readers. Hungry alpha males are her calling card, and the wilder the men, the more she'll make them pour their hearts out. She werebear swears there'll be no swooning heroines in her books. It takes tough-as-nails women to handle her shifters.

Experienced at handling an alpha male of her own, she lives in a tiny town, outside of a tiny city, and devotes her life to writing big stories. Foodie, wolf whisperer, ninja, thief of tiny bottles of awesome smelling hotel shampoo, nap connoisseur, movie fanatic, and zombie slayer, and most of this bio is true.

Bear Shifters? Check
Smoldering Alpha Hotness? Double Check
Sexy Scenes? Fasten up your girdles, ladies and gents, it's gonna to be a wild ride.

For more information on T. S. Joyce's work,
visit her website at
www.tsjoyce.com